SURRENDERED IN SALEM

CASTERS & CLAWS

NEW YORK TIMES and USA TODAY
BESTSELLING AUTHOR

MILLY TAIDEN

Selene Bishop runs the Healsome Magic Center with her sister. She loves her job, but she did wish that her life had time for something more. She doesn't know what she's looking for, but she would settle from a bit of free time. When she is taken to a secluded house on a wolf's pack lands for her own safety, Selene realizes that she might have gotten exactly what she was hoping for.

Jett is a grumpy wolf who doesn't expect much out of life. After a lifetime of regrets, he's just fine being on his own. None of his plans include finding his mate. In fact, he is adamant that he doesn't want a mate. He just knows that domestic life isn't for him. He wants to work in the bar and go through the motions. But when he is sent to save a witch, he comes face to face with what he never wanted.

Selene might be a witch, but she understands the pull of the mate sense. She also has a lot of compassion for what Jett has been through. While he is protecting her from the Order of Salem, Selene is doing some saving of her own. Will she be able to mend her mate's broken heart or will they lose out on the love of a lifetime?

Published By
Latin Goddess Press, Inc.
Winter Springs, FL 32708
http://millytaiden.com
Spellstruck in Salem
Copyright © 2020 by Milly Taiden
Copyright by Latin Goddess Press, Inc.
Edited by: Tina Winograd
Cover: Jacqueline Sweet

—*For my readers,*

I hope you enjoy the last installment of our Salem witches. And I hope you all find your own happily ever after.

CHAPTER ONE

SELENE

Selene pushed the stack of sticky notes to a corner of the reception desk. The space was clear and organized, and that made her very happy. It wouldn't stay. She knew that. The second her sister sat behind the desk, there would be carnage on her thoughtfully organized work area.

Technically, it was *their* desk so Selene really shouldn't be so territorial and particular. But Astra sort of bred chaos wherever she went. Selene knew that was the fire magic inside her twin. It wasn't exactly Astra's fault.

But it sure drove Selene insane. Needing to do something to keep busy before her pride and joy, *Healsome Magic Holistic Center*, opened, she grabbed the office phone. It was either make a call or reorganize the pens. She'd done it twice already this morning, and she had a feeling that if she went for a third, she would end up feeling *way* guilty about her need to have everything *just* so. At least she was comforted to know this neurosis didn't follow her in her regular life. Just her work life, and that was enough, thank you very much.

There was one person in particular Selene needed to speak with. She dialed the number by memory.

"Are you awake yet?" Selene didn't even bother to hide the smile in her voice. Cerise, one of her cousins and half of another set of Bishop twins, would know she was being teased.

"What is the matter with you?" Cerise grumbled on the other line. "Who calls anymore? Can't you just text like a normal person?"

"So you can ignore me for a few hours? Absolutely not. I want to talk to you about expanding both of our businesses."

This was a project near and dear to her heart. Selene was desperate to merge and expand both *Gemstones* and *Healsome Magic Holistic Center*.

It would mean they could hire a few staff members and get the chance to take a day off.

Selene hadn't had one of those in so long, it made her ache. She loved her job, and she loved her business. But sometimes a lady just needed to stay in gross, ratty, and perfectly comfortable pajamas all day to play board games and watch movies.

That sounded like absolute heaven.

"I already told you that we have to get Raven in on this first," Cerise answered with a sigh. "We both know Raven will want a business plan and an idea of the profit margin. If we do some of the legwork before we talk to her, she's more likely to be receptive. I still think it's too soon to take this to her.

"I know she talks about wanting an expansion for both the store and your clinic, but if she puts all of her energy in this right now, she's going to be lost to the business forever. She'll let it consume her. I want to wait until she's over Arthur."

Selene scoffed. "Fuck that guy. I think this is the best thing for her."

And she really believed that. Focusing on something new would be good for her cousin and good for business.

"Give me a few more weeks, and then we can start on the business plan for the expansion. I'll do some recon and see what Raven would want, that way she can't say no to us."

"I hate that you're right," Selene mumbled.

If anyone knew how to wrangle Raven into doing things she didn't like doing, it was Cerise. Raven was, without a doubt, the most stubborn of all four Bishops.

"It's because I'm older and wiser than you," Cerise teased.

Selene rolled her eyes, and she hoped the cousin could sense it even at a distance.

"Look, witch," Selene said, "let's reconvene in three weeks. I have to go. Astra isn't here yet and her client has just arrived."

"Creepy Mrs. Gellar?"

"Yup," Selene confirmed. "I still say she's evil."

Not that Selene would ever admit that to Astra. It was bad enough her twin believed it. Selene didn't need to feed into the paranoia.

"Oh, come off it. She's an innocent little old lady. She's what, eighty?"

"Probably more like two-hundred. I seriously think she's a vampire."

"Okay, Selene. This is where I let you go if you're going to go all conspiracy on me."

Selene put the receiver down just as Mrs. Gellar walked in.

"I don't like your door," the woman snapped. "It's too damn heavy."

"I'm sorry about that. You could use the mechanical feature, if you'd like."

Mrs. Gellar gave her a cold stare down and Selene had to force herself not to shiver.

"Is she here yet, or am I going to have to make small talk with you?" Mrs. Gellar sat in one of the chairs in the small waiting area and tapped her watch.

She was a few minutes early, not that it would matter to Mrs. Gellar.

"You look tired. Not going to catch a husband with bags under your eyes." Mrs. Gellar gave her another pointed onceover. "Or that haircut."

Instinctively, Selene's hand went to her hair. She lowered her hand, hoping the gesture hadn't been spotted. Mrs. Gellar was being particularly snippy. Selene felt bad for Astra. It was obviously not going to be a good session. And afterward? Selene would have to deal with a very grumpy and very short-tempered Astra. She could only hope that she would have time to do her morning ritual.

It was an important part of her day, one that

made her ready to take on whatever events might occur.

"Are your parents and uncle and aunt still off on trips like a bunch of teenagers?" Mrs. Gellar pulled an antibacterial wipe from her purse and began to rub the chair's arms. "It's disgraceful for people their age to go off gallivanting like that."

Selene was seething. No one dissed her parents, or her family, for that matter. She was proud of all four of them for moving to a sunnier place. They were always off visiting all types of different countries, going on adventures. Selene knew those experiences would keep the four aging members of her family young for a while.

"I admire them," she said with a shrug. "I'd love to travel one day." She meant it, too. She loved Salem, and she really didn't think she'd ever move from her hometown, and she was more a homebody than she cared to admit. She wished she had that travel bug.

There was a want to travel, and then actually doing it. Selene knew she would probably always be in the first category.

"Tsk. Admire them."

Astra chose that particular moment to burst through the door. Selene didn't miss the new rose quartz necklace around her neck. She shook her head and made a mental note to stop by *Gemstones* to pay for the piece of jewelry. Knowing her twin, Astra hadn't paid for it.

"Morning, Mrs. Gellar," her sister's chipper tone was fake and forced. The corner of her smile was slightly downturned, like it was hurting her to smile, while the warmth didn't reach her eyes. "If you'll just follow me to Room 2."

"Room 3," Selene corrected.

"Right. That's the one."

Mrs. Gellar stood and started walking down the hall.

"Be good," Selene mouthed to Astra, but she shook her head with large wide eyes.

It was an interesting task, keeping her sister in line. Selene was used to it, but that didn't mean it wasn't exhausting. Thank god coffee and carbs existed to help her carry on.

Selene felt like a rebel as she waited to duck out of the shop on a mission for her morning treat. She, too, could be the rebellious twin.

CHAPTER TWO

JETT

Jett Arrowood had made many mistakes in his life. Many. More than most people. In fact, Jett knew his life was nothing more than one long string of bad decisions. That wasn't just his opinion. The entire wolf pack had the same impression of him.

And he had gone and proved them right. Again.

He didn't want to move, nor did he want the woman in his bed to move. If everything just stopped for one second, he could go on pretending that last night hadn't happened. Sure, he could be a major jackass, but he could stay right as he was and not feel like the biggest asshole in the world for a few more seconds.

"You awake?" his bedmate snuggled into his

side and Jett had to fight his instincts to not shove her away.

He knew Leah was bad news for him, just like he knew he shouldn't have brought her home last night. At the very least, nothing had happened. He had pretended to be too drunk, but Leah had insisted on sleeping over. She'd purred into his ear that he could make up for it in the morning.

Now that it was bright out and the sun was streaming into his bedroom, he wanted to send her packing and pretend this had never happened. Jett had decided he would stop fucking around. That he would clean up his act. But apparently, old habits died hard.

At first, his lady-killer, bad-boy attitude had been a facade he took on because that was what the wolf pack expected of an Arrowood. Somewhere along the way, it had stopped being an act, and Jett thought the only happiness he deserved, the only kind of joy he could ever be worth, was the five-second relief of emptying his balls into his flavor of the week. That wasn't a pretty thought. And he sure as shit wasn't proud of it.

But Jett hadn't had the greatest role model and he hadn't exactly been given a fair shot. That's what happened when your mom bailed and dad went into lockup for a double homicide.

"I'm awake," he told Leah, hoping she would go on her merry way. He didn't want to tell her she had to go, but it would have been nice if she had gotten to that conclusion all on her own.

There was already a lot of self-hatred going on in his brain, and he didn't need any more than he was dealing with.

"Don't you want to pick up where we left off last night?" she purred as she ran a long red claw down in his chest.

"No," he sat up and swung his legs off the bed.

If there had been an easy way to get rid of Leah, Jett would have used it. As it was, he was caught between telling her to fuck off and trying to be nice. Why the hell had he brought her home? He could have chosen any other woman, but nope. Jett Arrowood, in all of his idiot greatness, had to pick the woman who always wanted to be with him.

His phone began to vibrate angrily on the bedside table. He looked down at the screen and saw it was his alpha. Considering they had been together only four hours ago at the bar were they worked, Jett knew he wasn't exactly being saved by the bell. There was trouble brewing. He could feel it in his bones.

"What's up, Alpha?" His voice was heavy with sleep and he coughed to clear it.

"You need to get your ass out of bed. I'll be by in ten minutes to discuss a few things with you."

"Can't we do this over the phone?" Jett really didn't want Blaze to see Leah had spent the night. He didn't need the added guilt trip.

"Ten minutes," Blaze warned.

Jett hung up the phone and retreated to the bathroom. He took a quick shower, and once he was done, he only had a few minutes to convince Leah to stay in the house until he was gone. She took serious offense to the fact that Jett didn't want the alpha to know she was there.

"You're the worst," she told him, rolling over in the bed. Her clothes were all rumpled from sleep. "I can't believe you try so hard to seem like a decent guy. The whole pack knows you're a piece of shit, Jett Arrowood."

His jaw tensed at Leah's words. Jett knew she wasn't wrong, but it didn't make it any easier to hear. He slammed the bedroom door, making sure to have his phone and wallet in his pockets.

Blaze, the alpha to his enforcer, was already

waiting for him in his driveway. Jett muttered a curse, hoping Blaze wouldn't smell Leah on him. He didn't need his alpha to be disappointed in his behavior again.

The reality was that he and Blaze had been friends since they were kids. He had never been judged by him, nor did Blaze ever give any credence to the bullshit the others spewed about Jett. Not even when Jett managed to get them into trouble.

That was probably why Blaze had chosen him as his first enforcer. Not just out of loyalty, but also because Jett knew trouble. He understood and knew how to wade through it. It also made him the best bouncer *Gray Wolf* had ever had. The shifter bar Blaze ran was where Jett had picked up Leah the night before at the very end of his work shift.

"Why in the fuck do we need to be up so early?" Jett grumbled.

Because in an ideal world, Jett would have woken up, sent Leah packing and slept all day until it was time to go to work. He enjoyed his job at *Gray Wolf*, but he also liked his sleep.

"Got a call from Axel," Blaze explained. "There's trouble brewing up there in Salem."

Jett rubbed at his eyes, hoping to make blinking less painful.

"How is that our problem?" Jett didn't mean to snap at his alpha, but waking up next to Leah hadn't put him in a good mood.

"This group of witch hunters calling themselves the Order of Salem are after some women. Axel called to warn us. He thinks it might splash onto our lands."

"Witch hunters?"

"Right. Witch hunters. Apparently, these idiots want to kill the descendants of all the Salem witches executed during the Salem trials. In the same order and everything."

"Didn't a bunch of witch families leave Salem to settle here after the trials?" Jett was interested despite himself and his shitty morning.

"Yup. And it just so happens that two of the first intended victims basically live on the border between Salem and Marblehead."

"So what are we going to do? Stop an assassination attempt on two witches?"

"That's right. Axel and Zane are taking care of two witches of their own. The two women we have to help are a set of twins, Astra and Selene Bishop. They own a holistic center in Salem. I'll head over there while you go to their place. We need to keep them in separate locations. That way the witch hunters are spread thin. It'll give our pack, the Salem pack, *and* the Salem sheriff's office the chance to catch all of them before anyone is hurt."

"Lucky for us the Salem sheriff is a wolf enforcer of his own pack."

Blaze opened his mouth, but snapped it shut, his features darkening. Jett didn't have to turn around to know exactly what had pissed off his alpha.

Jett had purposefully told Leah to stay in the house until he was gone. Of course, she hadn't listened. She was barefoot and clearly wearing the same clothes she had on at the bar the previous night. She stumbled on her feet when she saw them. Like she didn't know they were there.

"Oh. Hi, Alpha," she mumbled with feigned embarrassment.

"Hey, Leah," he answered.

As soon as she drove off, Jett could feel Blaze's eyes on him.

"Don't say anything. Nothing happened. I was too drunk." That wasn't a lie, but it wasn't the truth either. He hoped the alpha didn't pick up on it.

"You gotta stop fucking around, Jett. For real. How do you expect to be ready for your real mate if you're wasting all of your time sleeping around?"

Jett shrugged. "I'm not looking for my mate. You know that. We can't all be stand up men like you. I'm not meant for the wife and kids thing."

His alpha shook his head like he wanted to say something but he didn't. Jett didn't want to know what he was thinking. He figured it was something about how fucked up his parents were.

Blaze said, "Back to our business. We'll keep the witches separate, and once all of the culprits have been stopped, then we'll let them go about their business."

"Fine. So I'm to bring the witch here?" Jett asked.

"Yes. Keep her safe and, please, I beg you. Do not fuck her. We don't need things to get complicated."

Jett sighed and crossed his arms. "Really? You think it's necessary to warn me not to have sex with a woman I'm protecting?"

"Well," Blaze pointed in the direction Leah had disappeared. "Can you blame me?"

"Like I said, nothing happened. We stumbled

home drunk, that's it. Not that who I fuck is any of your business."

"But it is. You're my enforcer and how you behave is a direct reflection of me and my leadership. You need to chill out, Jett. I get that you don't want to fall in love again after what happe—"

"I'm not doing this." Jett walked around to his car. "I've got a witch to save. Text me the address."

"Jett," Blaze called out, "keep me posted. Let me know when you get back here with one of the witches."

"Yes, Alpha." There was an edge of attitude to Jett's voice.

It wasn't insubordination. He simply knew Blaze expect more of him, and now he had let him down again.

CHAPTER THREE

SELENE

S elene was almost bouncing on her feet as she watched Astra follow Mrs. Gellar into one of the treatment rooms. She looked at the clock and knew she had about fifty-seven minutes to go to the cafe down the street, grab her breakfast and enjoy it quietly before Astra was done with her appointment.

It wasn't so much that Selene didn't like sharing a house with her twin sister. It was more because Selene wanted a bit of peace and quiet while she enjoyed her coffee and Danish. No. She didn't want that. She *needed* that.

There wasn't enough coffee in the world to deal with a grumpy Astra, and her twin would be extra grumpy with a small dash of bitchy as soon as her appointment with Mrs. Gellar was done. Astra was a great Reiki master, and she could almost work miracles.

It's not like Mrs. Gellar could get Reiki healing anywhere else in town. She'd have to drive all the way to Boston for the other natural healing center.

Astra had to deal with it, and in turn, Selene had to deal with it.

And she dealt with it with large amounts of coffee and the warmest, bestest cheese Danishes in the entire world.

Selene all but skipped to the cafe. The morning sun was making the glass storefronts glimmer. Salem was such a beautiful little town. It was full of charm, and even though her people's history here was complicated, Selene didn't think she would ever leave this place. It was homey and far removed from the loud, boisterous mess that Boston was.

Not that there was anything wrong with the city. Selene was a small-town girl who had grown up to love the quieter pace a place like Salem could offer.

Selene checked her phone. She still had forty-minutes. *Plenty* of time.

The line in the coffee shop was longer than

other mornings, which meant someone else was there. There was a very tall, very muscular man standing at the counter waiting to be served. The barista, a tiny little dude named Lester, was struggling with the steamer this morning. Selene was used to it when the teen opened the cafe for his parents.

Mr. Tall and Grumpy ahead of her didn't seem to understand that. He let loose his twentieth sigh in ten seconds.

"Hey, Lester," Selene said with a warm smile. "How's the morning going?"

She knew if she was kind and sweet with Lester, that whatever the mean costumer said wouldn't matter. She would outsmart meanness with niceness.

"Oh, Selene. Hey. Give me a second. This thing is on the fritz again."

Selene muttered a spell under her breath. It was a small simple one that would give Lester the confidence to tackle whatever problem the steamer was giving him.

"Look, kid. I just want a coffee and one of those." The man pointed to the glass display where all of the delicious baked goods were displayed.

21

"Just one moment," Lester answered. "I have to f—"

"No, I don't have time. I'm on the clock. This is kind of life or death. Just pour me a black coffee and give me one of those and I'll be on my way."

"Life or death?" Selene wanted to bite her tongue for saying that so loudly. What had possessed her to say *anything*?

Mr. Tall and Grumpy turned to face her. *Oh, mama.* She nearly swallowed her tongue. He was so hot, so sexy, that she forgot what she had said.

"Excuse me?" he asked her. His soft brown eyes shaded to something much darker, but Selene stood her ground. She wasn't going to let herself be intimidated by a hot dude. Especially not if said hunk was being a complete dick to poor little Lester.

Selene shook her head. "Be nice. No one is in that much of a rush. Unless you're a doctor on a call—"

He sure didn't look like a doctor. He looked like an angry lumberjack who hadn't been around other humans in a very long time.

"Did you just tell me to be *nice*?" he asked. His voice was rough and low like he didn't use it very often. It definitely reinforced Selene's belief that the man rarely spoke to others. Angry lumberjack indeed.

She would teach him some manners. Selene opened her mouth to respond, but Mr. Tall and Grumpy was watching something over her shoulder. She didn't even have time to turn and see what had his sexy face in a scowl.

"Drop the gun," Mr. Tall and Grumpy growled. Like an *actual* growl. It was a primal, dangerous sound that made Selene nervous.

She opened her mouth to state she *obviously* didn't have a gun. Was he even well? Hallucinating, maybe.

That's when the impossible happened.

The man in front of her shrank into a large black wolf. Selene didn't know what to do, so she decided to faint.

CHAPTER FOUR

JETT

Fuck *this.* Jett rubbed his chin again, wanting nothing more than to jump over the counter and pour his own damn cup of coffee. This kid was taking his sweet ass time, playing around with a machine he clearly didn't understand.

His impatience was growing by the second. He shouldn't have stopped for coffee. If something happened to the witch, Blaze was going to gut him like a fish. But Jett was feeling the effects of no sleep and he also knew that if he had to have patience with his rescue, he would have to have a decent amount of caffeine running through his blood.

Jett was contemplating actually climbing over the counter when the bell over the door dinged.

All of the air left the room in one sudden *whoosh*. It felt like he had been body-checked. He couldn't quite understand why his lungs were burning with the need to take in even more air. He was panting, unable to get what he needed.

Mate.

Fuck. No.

Mate. Turn around. We can smell her.

There was no way in hell Jett was going to turn around now. He didn't want a mate. He was fine being by himself. This had to be some kind of mistake. His wolf was only confused because they were tired and hadn't had any coffee yet.

Jett was on a mission to rescue a witch from a bunch of lunatics. He didn't have time to get all torn up about some chick.

His animal took serious offense to that thought and thrashed against his mind. The beast wanted to set his eyes upon their mate; Jett wanted to pretend such things didn't exist. What were the chances of him walking into a cafe he saw in Salem and coming face to face with his mate? Slim to none.

Turn. Around. Now.

The wolf was persistent, but Jett was in control. He clenched his jaw until his teeth made a painful grinding sound. He'd have a headache later. His hands balled into fists at his side. He just needed coffee. Then this would all be much easier to deal with.

"Hey, Lester. How's the morning going?" the woman asked from *right* behind him.

Jett and his wolf were in total disagreement about the sound of her voice. The animal was all but purring that it was lovely, but Jett was intent on finding it irritating. It had made the hair on his neck rise. That had to be a bad thing. It had to be.

"Oh, Selene." The kid behind the counter blushed and his hands began shaking. "Hey. Give me a second. This thing is on the fritz again." It was clear the little dude had a crush on his wolf's mate. But Jett still found it aggravating. Now the barista would be even more nervous, and he wouldn't get my coffee.

"Look, kid," Jett said, his throat feeling like sandpaper. He was trying very hard not to sound like a complete animal. He would leave that up to his wolf. "I just want a coffee and one of those." The cheese Danish was calling his name. His wolf

27

might want to eat up the woman behind him, but Jett just wanted the pastry.

"Just one moment," the worker stumbled on his words, making Jett sigh. "I have to f—"

He didn't have time for this. If his alpha, Blaze, knew that Jett had stopped somewhere for coffee instead of going directly to save the witch, the other wolf would skin him alive. Jett wasn't disobeying an order. He just knew he would be more pleasant with whomever it was he was meant to rescue.

Not that Jett was ever pleasant. He was an asshole, and he knew it. His exchange with Leah that morning had only served to prove that.

"No." Jett was throwing daggers at the kid. "I don't have time. I'm on the clock. This is kind of life or death. Just pour me a coffee and give me one of those and I'll be on my way." He pointed to the display case, but he no longer cared what he got, so long as he could cram food down his throat.

Maybe he could chew loudly enough to drown out his wolf's bitching and moaning. The animal was doing his head in, repeating he needed to turn around so that they could finally gaze upon their mate.

"Life or death?" the woman asked from behind

him. There was a bite to her words. Like she didn't believe him.

"Excuse me?" he asked her, turning to face her, despite himself.

Oh. Shit.

She was hot.

Not just hot, but downright perfect.

Mate, his wolf was chanting. *Ask her out. Buy her a coffee. She smells good. Sniff her.*

Jett tightened his jaw, but he couldn't stop himself from staring at her. Her blonde hair barely reached her shoulders and there was a cute little wave to it, like she had spent her day at the beach. Jett narrowed his eyes, sure the wolf inside him was the one noticing how gorgeous the curvy woman was even in her black scrubs.

To her credit, she didn't even seem fazed by his death glare. Figures his mate would be mismatched to him.

"Be nice," she commanded, making him bristle.

Had she really just given him an order? Why did that amuse him? She said, "No one is in that much of a rush. Unless you're a doctor on call—"

He was being admonished. By a stranger. By his mate. He was so surprised, it took a few seconds for his brain to catch up. "Did you just tell me to be *nice?*" he asked.

If his mate answered his question, Jett never heard it. All of his attention was on the small group of people coming toward the cafe. He could see their determined advance through the large window. They had guns and mean looks on their faces.

It was one of two things.

Either the armed people were going to hold up a small-town cafe, or they were there for the witch. Jett was willing to bet that these people were the witch hunters Blaze had warned him about. How lucky for him they had found him.

The bell jingled cheerfully as they came in. Jett wasted no time making his presence known.

"Drop the gun," he said to the lot of them.

He wasn't surprised when they didn't.

As Jett was figuring out a plan to get the hell out of there, his brain finally caught up. The kid had called the blonde woman Selene. That could only mean she was the witch he was meant to rescue, and those fuckers armed to the teeth were the witch hunters.

Logically, Jett knew he shouldn't shift in front of all of these humans. But there were two men and one woman pointing guns at his mate. His wolf took over, and Jett shifted right there in public and in full view of a handful of humans.

He growled at the attackers, and he hoped Selene would move away.

She didn't.

She'd fainted. The woman had actually passed out. Her body was crumpled on the floor, making her a very easy target.

For fuck's sake. Of course, the witch he had to rescue was his mate. Of course, she was full of fake courage, telling strangers to be nice. Of course, she fainted when she saw guns.

And a supposed human turn into a wolf.

CHAPTER FIVE

JETT

Jett's wolf eyes were glued to the three intruders, waiting for one of them to do *something*. He stood in front of his mate, sizing each of them up. There was a second gun, more likely a handgun, tucked next to the bald man's leg. The woman had a large knife strapped to her thigh. The last witch hunter, a rotund man, didn't seem to be carrying any weapons, but Jett knew looks could be deceiving.

"You can't have guns in here," the kid behind the counter stammered. One of his hands was pointing at the two men and one woman accusingly. The other was fumbling with something, and Jett hoped to fuck the kid had enough sense to call the cops.

The large man laughed. The throaty sound was aggravating to Jett's wolf ears.

"This doesn't concern you, kid," the man said between two more chuckles. "Just go about your business and forget we were ever here."

Jett was kind of hoping the barista's crush on Selene would light a fire under his ass. Usually, Jett wouldn't mind fighting off three bigoted humans, but they were armed with shotguns and who knew how desperate they would get.

"Pick her up," the woman instructed the two men as she pointed the barrel of her gun at Jett.

Jett growled loudly and menacingly at them. They were not taking his mate away to do god knew what to her. He was going to stop them if it was the last thing he did. Not because she was his mate, though that helped. Nope. It was strictly about doing what was right.

Taking stock of the situation and the cramped space they were in, Jett felt like a trapped animal. He couldn't launch himself at them since the cafe was so small. He had to snap at their legs, snarling as he avoided the butt of one gun and a few kicks.

"Just shoot the fucker," the woman called out.

"He's a wolf," one of her companions said.

"Imagine how pleased the boss will be if we manage to get a witch and a wolf."

While the woman pondered this, Jett took his chance. He lunged forward on his agile paws and bit into the bald man's leg. Blood filled his mouth and he tugged at the flesh, doing significant damage. He wasn't entirely sure if he had nicked an artery, but when the man fell to the ground, he was quickly circled by a large pool of blood. Jett spat out a large chuck of material and skin, refusing to swallow the vile piece of witch hunter.

The woman aimed at Jett and fired. He narrowly dodged the shot spewing from the shell. As she was working to aim at him again, Jett kept moving. He was banking on her having bad aim, and moving targets were always harder to nail down. It wasn't like he could stand guard over Selene's body. He was scared that if he was too close, spray from the blast would hit her.

Shit, he was doing a piss poor job of protecting her.

At least he had been at the cafe to intercept the attack. Had he not stopped for coffee, Selene would have been gone. Long before he even knew she had been taken. It was quite the coincidence he had decided to get coffee before going on his mission.

Jett's mind was reeling as he dodged another shot. Now the woman had to reload her shotgun or use her knife. Jett was going for the large man and he would deal with the big knife after.

Sliding on the waxed linoleum floor, Jett skidded as he tried to launch himself at the witch hunter. A shot rang out, making his ears buzz. He was shaking his head to regain his composure when he saw the kid leaving the safety of the counter with a large silver pitcher in his hands.

With a loud grunt, the boy threw the contents of the pitcher toward the second man. The witch hunter immediately dropped his gun, his hands going to his face. It wasn't until Jett saw the man's burning, steaming red skin that he caught on. The barista had just thrown boiling water at the attackers. Jett was pleasantly surprised by the balls it had taken to do that. He yipped encouragingly in the kid's direction as he gritted his teeth at the woman.

The boy grabbed the fallen gun and pointed it from one attacker to the other.

"I-I've c-called the cops," he said with a squeaky, terrified voice. "You seriously messed up my parents' shop and they are going to k-kill me when they see this. So unless you want to d-die, I s-suggest you drop your w-weapons."

The woman cackled and lunged toward the kid with the knife. Terrified, the kid fired, shattering glass. Jett saw this as his chance. He bounded onto a table and threw himself at the woman. With the weight of him knocking her back, she fell to the ground. Jett snapped at her face, but her screams of terror were enough for him. She wouldn't cause any more trouble for the time being.

Off in the distance, the sirens of the incoming cop cars were a relief. But Jett had to grab Selene and go. He knew the sheriff's office in Salem was mostly wolf shifters and their enforcer was the one who had orchestrated this rescue mission for all the Bishop witches, but he had to leave. On the off chance that the officers who showed up weren't in on the gig, he needed to get the witch to safety.

Jett shifted back into his human form and tried to put on what remained of his pants. They were ripped and in pretty bad shape, but at least he could cover his junk. Shifters were one hundred percent all right with nudity, but the barista was about a second away from joining Selene in the land of the unconscious, so Jett thought it would be best if he tried to dress himself.

"Think you can handle them until the cops get here? They must be only a minute out."

The kid nodded. "I-I think so. What are you going to do with Selene?"

Jett looked down at the woman who was still passed out. His wolf was overjoyed that its mate was safe, but Jett wasn't looking forward to taking her to his home. That was the order he'd been given by his alpha. Now that he knew who Selene was, it felt like an imposition.

It was too intimate, and it would only serve to confuse his wolf. He couldn't have that.

"I'm taking her someplace safe," Jett answered the kid.

The young man looked unsure. "Shouldn't you stay here and give the cops your statement?"

"You can give them my number." Jett jotted it down on a napkin and tossed it to the kid. "I'm working with Axel, the sheriff, so it's all good." Jett watched the young man take the napkin. Sweat rolled off him. It smelled almost as bad as his raging anxiety. "Don't worry about her," he tipped his chin in Selene's direction. "I'll take good care of her."

His wolf would sure make certain of that.

"You did good, kid. You were really brave."

The barista gave him a small smile as if he wasn't used to being complimented. It made Jett feel bad for earlier when he had all but chewed out the kid for being slow with the milk steamer.

Jett slid on his shirt which was a torn mess, but better than nothing. It took very little effort to pick up Selene. He tried not to get caught up by the fact she was in his arms. Her curves were all soft and subtly calling his name. Her scent tickled his nose. It was a mix of vanilla and brown sugar, and it made his mouth water. She smelled like the most delicious treat.

But she was one delectable looking snack.

He was going to have a hell of a time trying to resist her.

CHAPTER SIX

SELENE

Selene had the sudden urge to run, but she didn't know why. Her eyes were firmly closed and refused to open. She was seconds away from panicking, and her breath kept catching. Her mind swirled as she tried to remember just what the hell had made her so upset.

She had been at her favorite cafe. The cheese Danish she had so been craving was only a few feet away from her, locked in its display case. There had been Lester, struggling with the steamer. And Mr. Tall and Grumpy.

Oh.

Then she remembered.

The irate stranger had turned into a wolf. The

man had actually disappeared to be replaced by a large black wolf with very intense brown eyes. Selene couldn't quite remember anything after that. She had the sneaking suspicion she had fainted.

It had happened before when she was a little girl and her cat had almost been run over by a car. The way her head felt all woozy and her body had refused to cooperate then, too. It also happened every now and again when her blood sugar levels dipped between a certain level.

She slowly opened her eyes to realize she was in a speeding truck. Mr. Tall and Grumpy was at the wheel in ripped clothes. Selene tried to blink away the illusion. She must have taken a hit to the head if she was having a hallucination this real about being kidnapped. She pinched herself, hoping to snap out of it. Instead of waking her, it hurt like a bitch.

That could only mean one thing.

She was actually in a stranger's truck while he drove at top speeds through a residential area.

"Where the hell are you taking me?" Her voice echoed through the small cab of the truck.

Her captor played with the radio knob and the music lowered to a hum in the background. He looked at her for a few seconds, but his eyes returned on the road.

"Who are you?" Selene demanded.

For one wild second, she thought about opening the truck door to throw herself out, but that was a little bit too crazy. She could die or get seriously hurt. Instead, she plastered herself to the door, trying to stay as far away from the man who had taken her as possible.

Selene blinked at him a few times and she was really hoping he wouldn't turn into a wolf again. They'd crash and die. She didn't want to be his captive, but she didn't want to die either.

"I'm Jett Arrowood. I just saved your life, so maybe try not to yell at me."

"You didn't save me," she shouted, "you kidnapped me. And before I was able to get my cheese Danish."

"You passed out, so you missed what happened back there."

Selene shook her head. At least she *had* passed out. That explained why she hadn't had the chance to defend herself against her attacker.

"Well?" she snapped, hoping her fake courage was enough to intimidate the man, "are you going to tell me what happened?"

"Do you know who the Order of Salem is?"

Selene shook her head. It sounded vaguely familiar, but she didn't know why. "What does the Order of Salem have to do with anything?"

"Right. They're a group of witch hunters. They have it in their heads to kill off the Salem witches in the same order in which they were killed back in 1692. And the Bishops…"

"Were the first to die," Selene interrupted. "Yes, I know. But witches aren't real."

She tried to inject confidence and assuredness in her voice. It wasn't easy. She was still shaking from having passed out. And she was still half-expecting Jett to turn into a wolf and drive them off the road. Shit, what kind of morning had she stumbled into?

"Just like wolf shifters aren't real," Jett shot back, giving her a side glance.

"Wol-wolf shifters?"

Well, fuck. That explained why Jett had turned into a wolf in the cafe. He was a wolf shifter. Selene had never seen one in person, but she had definitely heard of them. She felt silly for not catching on earlier that she had witnessed a shifter transform into its animal. She shook her head, trying to clear her thoughts.

"I know it's a lot to handle," Jett said. "But we exist."

"Right. You're a shifter and you stopped the Order of Salem from killing me. I have two questions. First, why the hell did you save me? I'm a witch, not a shifter. And second, how in the fuck did you learn about their plans to kill me?"

Selene didn't even want to know what would have happened to her if Jett hadn't intervened and shifted into his wolf.

"How *did* you save me? I didn't see. You said *guns*, and then I—"

"Whoa, Selene. I can only do so much talking, and you're talking way too fast for me to catch up. Let me just get through this, okay?"

Selene nodded, and Jett went on to explain how the Order of Salem had a member who had ratted out the others to the sheriff. Selene was surprised to know the Salem sheriff's office was comprised of mostly wolf shifters. But at least the wolves had decided to help and intervene on the witches' behalf.

No one had done that during the witch trials that had nearly decimated Selene's ancestors.

"We're four wolves, two alphas and their

enforcers. Each one of us has one of you. Your sister and your two cousins."

"Are they okay?" She felt very shaky again, and the edge of her mind began to slip as she thought of what could have happened to her family members.

"Far as I can tell, yes. We can give my alpha, Blaze, a call when we get back to the pack lands up in Marblehead."

"Marblehead?" Selene was shocked. "Why would the Marblehead wolf pack be involved?"

"Because you and your sister share a house on the border between Salem and Marblehead. And also, because back after the witch trials, a lot of the Salem witches came to settle in Marblehead. We figured it would only be a matter of time before the Order of Salem came onto our lands."

With another nod, Selene focused on the fast moving scenery outside the window. It was a lot to process is such a short amount of time.

"And how exactly do we plan on taking down these witch killers?"

Jett tightened his grasp on the steering wheel. "The sheriff's deputies are taking care of it, both in Salem and Marblehead. Both wolf packs are also helping out because this is a paranormal problem.

The only issue is that the threat is human, so both alphas want to deal with it in the perimeters of human laws."

"Your tone is telling me that you would have handled it differently."

"Absolutely. These judgmental people want only to destroy witches because you're different, right? Way I see it, they don't even deserve to breathe air."

Selene bristled. "That's a bit harsh. I mean, they haven't hurt anyone yet, right? Maybe they would chicken out?"

"They had three people come to kill you, heavily armed. If it hadn't been for that kid throwing boiling water on them, you and I would be lying dead on the floor of that cafe. They're not innocent until proven guilty, Selene. They are definitely guilty. The intent was there."

She didn't want to think about that or believe it. How could strangers want to kill her simply because of her last name? Simply because she could do a little bit of magic?

If she was honest with herself, it made sense. The Bishop witches had been killed before. Her ancestor Rebecca had been a great healer, but when her magic had failed to heal the right

47

people, the town had turned on her. On all of the witches.

It was just history repeating itself.

Suddenly, all Selene wanted to do was hug her twin sister and watch a bunch of movies to forget that the real world was real. Her vision was swimming, and she clutched her head. She really didn't want to pass out again.

"Oh shit. You're kind of pale." There was real concern in Jett's voice.

"I haven't eaten in a little while and I have low-blood sugar."

"Fuck. Don't pass out again. I don't want to have to take you to the emergency room. What do I need to do to help?"

"I usually have a granola bar or something in my purse to…" she looked around the cab of the truck. "I don't seem to have it with me, though."

"Fuck. That's my bad. I didn't even think to grab it. I don't usually think about purses."

"It's okay. You wouldn't happen to have something I could quickly nibble on, do you?"

Jett shook his head, but Selene didn't miss the way he accelerated his driving speed. He pulled into a grocery store parking lot in Marblehead a few minutes later.

"Stay here," he instructed. "Don't pass out again. I'm going to get you some food."

Selene nodded, but she was already feeling dizzy and woozy. She was sure her first fainting spell of the day hadn't helped. She laid her head back and closed her eyes, hoping to stave off some of the nausea rolling around in her stomach.

"Here," Jett said as he hopped into the truck.

He handed her a small brown paper bag, and with shaking hands, Selene grabbed it. When she opened it, she gasped.

Inside of the bag was a small cheese Danish. She pulled it out, her eyes going up to him.

"Why did you grab this?" she asked him.

"Because you mentioned you like cheese Danishes. I figured this would be good. I also got this." He handed her a sports drink. "You might also want to drink this to get your electrolytes back up."

"Thanks," she whispered, bewildered. This action was so at odds with who Jett had seemed to be in the cafe, Selene didn't know what to think. She gulped down a few big mouthfuls of the sports drink before tearing into the Danish. The flaky crust was buttery against her tongue, and she rolled her eyes with a moan.

"Seriously, you're the sweetest." And she meant it, too. Selene ripped a corner of the pastry and handed it to Jett. "I guess you should have a piece of this since you also didn't get your coffee because of the attack."

Jett shot her a quick smile and shoved the bite into his mouth. "Thanks," he said as he cranked up the truck.

Selene tried to ignore the little flip her heart did when he smiled at her. He had been grumpy and irate a few moments ago. How could he pull a positive reaction from her now?

Oh, right. He had saved her life.

"So where are you taking me in Marblehead?" she asked to distract herself.

"You'll be staying with me. In my place. I'm on pack lands, so it's the safest place for you. The Order of Salem would have to be nuts to attack a wolf pack."

Selene nodded like she understood, but she didn't. Even as she ate and drank her breakfast, she felt anxiety gnawing at her insides. This was all too much to handle. How could she be sure anything Jett was saying was true? She had to talk to her sister. She had to know Astra was okay. When she told Jett as much, he promised they would call her as soon as they were safe in his home.

Selene took a deep breath and let the energy drink revitalize her.

This was fine. Everything was fine.

She had just been saved by a sexy man wolf. How much weirder could her day get?

CHAPTER SEVEN

JETT

As he drove to the edge of Marblehead where the pack lands met the ocean, Jett split his attention between the road and Selene. He had revealed a lot of information to her, and she had taken it in stride, but he could smell her anxiety. It was filling the cab and making his wolf angry. The animal wanted to be let out so he could try to console the witch, but Jett knew that made no sense. She would most likely pass out again.

Nope, he had to deal with this in his human form and he had to keep the mate stuff at a minimum. He wasn't going to seduce a witch who had been taken from everything and everyone she knew. That would make him an even bigger asshole than he already was.

He could go through this ordeal without ever telling Selene she was his mate. His wolf would just have to deal with it.

We'll see.

Jett turned onto pack land and drove the long stretch of road until he had to turn left to get to his house. Most of the pack lived to the right in a clustered community. He had taken a page out of his dad's book and holed up in an old cottage he had fixed up. He had distance from the bigger gossips of the pack, but he still had a piece of land and a house all his own.

When he finally parked in front of his house, Selene gasped.

"This is your house?" There was definitely doubt in her voice, and that irked Jett. "It's so cute."

What the fuck had she been expecting? A crack den? No, he knew how to keep a house. This property had been the first big purchase he had made, and he was proud of it. He took care of his little home. It was the first and only time he ever felt like he had a home, and he wasn't about to let the place rot away like he had let happen to his heart.

This house he would care about.

He tried to see it from Selene's perceptive. It was actually a very cute house. The siding was a pale blue and the door and shutters were white. It looked like a cottage from a fairy tale book he had seen when he was a kid. Maybe that's why he had bought it and fixed it up. Some small part of him, one he kept buried *way* down, was still holding onto the idea that maybe he deserved something nice.

"Yeah," was Jett's clipped response to Selene's question.

She hopped out of the truck, not even giving him the chance to open the door for her. He was still mildly concerned that she had passed out, and he wanted her to take things easy. A trip to the emergency room would have been difficult to explain to his alpha.

"Would you wait one fucking second?" he called out to her, hoping she was feeling steady on her feet. She seemed to be wobbling a bit.

Selene stopped on the stone pathway leading to the front door. Her arms were crossed, her shining blue eyes narrowed, and her foot was tapping lightly.

"I'm not going one step farther," she said.

"Just why the fuck not?" he asked, not able to contain the sharp edges of his tone.

Her eyes popped wide and her cheeks flushed.

"You need to either change your attitude or I'm leaving. I can find another wolf to protect me. One who is actually kind and nice. I don't need grumbled answers or being cussed out, do you hear me, Jett Arrowood?"

He swallowed against the tide of emotion in his throat. His wolf wasn't helpful in the slightest. The animal was furious with him for being so rude to his mate. But Selene was right. He did need an attitude change, or she should leave. She deserved a hell of a lot more than his grumpy, damaged ass. There was no way someone as beautiful and sweet as Selene Bishop was actually destined to be mated with the likes of him.

"I'm not used to having company," he said by way of explanation.

"Well, fine. But you can't swear at me and stomp around. If I'm supposed to stay with you until it's safe to go back to my regular life, can we at least try to make it as pleasant as possible?"

He gave her a small nod, but that wasn't enough. She wasn't budging.

"I'm sorry I yelled and swore at you." He

almost added that it was out of concern, but thought better of it. He didn't need to tell her that he didn't know how to care for another human being.

Jett opened the front door and motioned for Selene to go on ahead of him. She kicked off her shoes, and took a hesitant step forward. The entrance was a small little alcove that Jett had painted a dove gray color. The entryway led to the living room which had a clear view into the small but modern kitchen.

He had torn down a lot of the walls to make the small house more of an open-concept. It let in natural light and made it easier for him to watch the television from the breakfast nook in the kitchen.

Selene stood in the living room, looking around and soaking up all the details of his house. She gasped when she saw Bugsy. The large alcove took up a large corner of the living room. She rushed forward and lowered herself to the ground. She reached out her hand and dangled her fingers, making a soft calling noise.

She turned back to look at him, and her face was pulled into a confused frown.

"You have a pet bunny?"

Jett shrugged because he didn't know how else to react. Yup. He had a pet rabbit.

"But...you're a wolf. Don't wolves eat bunnies?"

Jett sighed, and he knew Selene wasn't going to let this go. It was better for him if he told her all about how Bugsy came into his life.

"When I was fixing this place up, I found a rabbit's nest near the back porch. Two of the other babies were dead, and this little guy was on the brink of starvation. I took him in, fed him. I had every intention of letting him go back out into the wild. But when he was healthy enough to go, I..."

He sniffed because he knew it wasn't exactly a macho story. "I couldn't let him go. He didn't have a mom or siblings to look out for him. He was all alone, and no one was going to show him the ways of the world."

He didn't add that he had felt a kinship with the abandoned bunny.

"How does the bunny not run away from you?"

"What do you mean?" he asked, genuinely confused by her question.

"Well, you're a predatory animal. I'm sure the rabbit's senses told him that. But why isn't he scared of you?"

"I don't know, maybe because he's used to me. I

fed him from the time he was a dying kit. He knows he has nothing to fear from me."

Unlike you, he wanted to add but thought better of it.

He would never hurt Selene. His wolf would never let him do that. But that didn't mean he wouldn't hurt her unintentionally if they ever *did* get together. Jett wasn't going to take that chance.

Having no-strings-attached hookups were just better.

"Can I pick him up?" she asked as Bugsy inched forward. He scratched his head against her fingers. Selene giggled and she shuffled closer.

"Yeah, he's actually quite cuddly."

He didn't need to tell her that he sometimes watched movies with Bugsy curled up on his chest. That wasn't something manly wolves did, and it wasn't something he was about to admit. It would give Selene the wrong impression. He wasn't the cuddly kind of guy that she should be hanging out with. Jett was still pretty fucking adamant that his wolf was wrong. This angel couldn't be his mate.

Selene picked Bugsy up and as soon as she cradled him to her chest, he lay his head against her shoulder, nuzzling her neck. *Lucky rabbit.* Jett wouldn't get to do that. Ever. But Bugsy sure seemed to be reveling in the attention Selene was giving him.

"I'm still so stunned you have a pet rabbit. You were so grumpy at the coffee shop. If I would have imagined you with any kind of animal, it would have been a snake or something."

"A snake?" he shook his head and suppressed a shudder at the idea of having a snake in the house.

"Not a fan of snakes?"

"Is anybody?" he asked.

The next thing he knew, he was standing right in front of Selene and his hand was reaching out to scratch Bugsy's fur. Jett felt pulled toward her, and his wolf was snickering in victory.

"I'm going to make coffee," he grumbled as he walked away.

He needed to remember that Selene was way out of his league. Even if she liked to play with his rabbit.

CHAPTER EIGHT

SELENE

S elene gently placed Bugsy back into his alcove. The bunny seemed reluctant to leave her arms, so she scratched his furry little head, promising him that she'd be back for more cuddles later on. Bugsy hopped off until he disappeared into a little house that was an identical replica of Jett's house. Selene didn't even have to ask. She instinctively knew Jett had built the small wooden structure for his little pal.

That was endearing.

From her vantage point in the living room, Selene could see Jett preparing a pot of coffee. If she put aside the way he had treated Lester in the cafe, and the way he had snapped at her outside of his house, Selene could admit he was indeed a fine male specimen. He was tall and wide in the best of ways. His sandy blond hair was cropped short, but that only put his brown eyes on display. His jaw was square, and even from the side, Selene could tell he was heartbreakingly handsome.

"Would you like some coffee instead of staring?"

If he hadn't turned to give her a smile, she would have thought the grumpy wolf was back. His smile made his eyes sparkle, and that just pulled her in. She made her way to the kitchen where he was taking the milk out of the fridge. Selene took it and noticed her hands were shaking.

The man was so sexy, it was making her nervous.

Nope.

She would have none of that. She was a badass witch, and she wasn't about to let a silly little crush on this stranger faze her.

Cup of coffee in hand, Selene made her way to the living room and she plopped herself onto the soft beige sofa. She sank right into it, and took a deep gulp of her drink. Her moan was completely accidental, but it earned her a look from Jett was who taking a seat at the farthest corner of the couch.

"I'm guessing, by that reaction, that the coffee is to your liking?"

"It is," she said before taking another large sip. "By this time, I usually have a couple of cups in my system. It's been kind of an insane morning."

"You're telling me," Jett agreed.

"So what happened...your alpha got the call from the Salem alpha and you all rode into town to save the day?"

Jett chuckled and shook his head. "Something like that. Though Blaze is a hell of a lot more gallant than me. I wasn't supposed to stop for coffee. I was meant to go straight to your house."

"Well, isn't it lucky you didn't? I don't think Lester and I could have taken on three armed witch hunters."

"Lester did all right."

"Isn't it insane that I'm here because I was under attack by witch hunters? Who am I supposed to trust after all this? I mean, I was just out for my breakfast, and *boom*." Selene smacked her hand against the sofa. "I'm being rescued. How does all of this even happen? Won't the pack be mad that your alpha has decided to get involved?"

"No, not in the slightest. If it means protecting the pack and its lands, they trust his judgment."

"But my family and I aren't part of the pack."

"You're supernatural beings being hunted. Don't think for a second they won't come after us now that they know we exist."

Yeah, that definitely was a surprise to her though it shouldn't have been. "Since we haven't been formally introduced," she put her hand out to him. "I'm Selene Bishop, co-owner of Healsome Magic Holistic Center. Nice to meet you."

His brow raised, but he took her hand in his large grip. "Right. I'm Jett Arrowood, pack enforcer. Same."

She rolled his eyes at his "same" remark instead of repeating her friendly greeting.

They finished the rest of their drinks in companionable silence. Selene's eyes kept sliding over to Jett. She was really surprised by the level of attraction she felt for him. It wasn't something she had ever experienced. She'd had only one relationship, and though Will had been cute, he had never made her hands shake or her breath catch.

Maybe Selene's particular brand of kink was grumpy wolves who saved her life.

"Okay. This silence is going to drive me crazy," Jett said as he took her empty cup of coffee. "Come on." He held out his hand for Selene to grab.

She furrowed her brow questioningly. "I thought you said we have to stay put? Where are we going?"

Jett rolled his eyes. "Stop being difficult for a second. You're on pack lands and you're being protected by the pack's main enforcer. You're safe here. But I would like to show you around the place. I would also like to introduce you to the pack. I think it would be good for you to know who has your back, but I think it would also be good for the pack to see you. That way they can feel more connected to you if something *were* to happen here on pack lands."

Selene blanched. "What do you mean, if something were to happen on pack lands? Do you really think the Order of Salem are going to attack us here?"

"Maybe, it's definitely a possibility. Not a likely one, because what kind of humans would like to go up against an entire pack of wolf shifters? But if it were to happen, I'd like for them to know who you are."

"Okay, I guess that makes sense."

"They're all right people. But they can also be judgmental."

Selene didn't miss the way his eyes darkened as

he spoke. There was something there. Selene knew that even if Jett was the pack's main enforcer, there was also a bit of tension between him and his people.

"Right, and because I'm a witch, they might not be so welcoming." She was guessing, but it was a decent guess.

"Something like that," he said with a shrug.

"Then I guess I'll just have to win them over." She gave him a big wide smile, and she hoped he would see it for what it was. She was going to make the people of the wolf pack love her, because that's exactly what she did.

Selene had never been hated by anyone. Not really. Actually, it was quite the opposite. Most people tended to like her; their ire usually was reserved for her twin sister who was slightly more aggressive and confrontational that Selene was.

"If you say so," Jett said.

He locked up the house behind them, earning him a look from Selene. "You'd think the pack enforcer's home would be safe on pack lands." She was teasing him, but he shook his head.

"I wouldn't bother locking it if you weren't staying with me. As it is, you are staying with me, and I kind of don't want anyone to sneak into the house and ambush us later."

Again, Selene felt the color drain from her face. "Is that really something we should be concerned about?"

Jett smiled. "No, not really. But if I let anything happen to you, I'll never hear the end of it."

His words felt heavy, almost like he was saying so much more. Selene searched his handsome face to see if she could understand his deeper meaning, but she couldn't.

Jett led her down a small sidewalk and he pointed to a few rows of houses. "That's where a few of the elders live with their families. They earned the ocean-front property after years of service to the pack."

They walked by a nice varnished-wood structure. The wood sparkled under the sun. The small sign in the front lawn read this was the Marblehead pack community center.

"What do you use this for?" Selene asked.

"We use it for pack meetings and for all kinds of different pack functions. There's a daycare center in there, too. A lot of the pack members prefer to have their little ones cared for by other wolves. Just in case a kid decides to go off and shift."

"You wouldn't want that at a normal, human daycare," Selene said with a smile.

"No, you wouldn't," he echoed.

"That makes me think of a time where my twin and I decided to do a bit of magic while we were in a daycare. I think we might have been six years old or so. Astra dared me to make the water in all of the juice boxes create a waterfall. She thought a red waterfall would be cool to see.

"I happened to think it was a very bad idea. I told her no, and I repeated it until she crossed her arms and tapped her foot at me. She basically told me there was no way I could do it. The little six-year-old doubted my magical ability, and so I wanted to prove to her I could actually do it. So what did I do? I did it.

"I made about twenty juice boxes explode and it created pure havoc. There was sticky fruit punch everywhere. The daycare worker couldn't understand how so many cardboard boxes had all exploded at once. But let me tell you, when Edith Bishop heard about the incident at pick-up that night, she knew exactly what had happened.

"My mother was furious with us. Of course, she

knew Astra had something to do with it. I had never been one to break rules, so Astra got more of my punishment than I did. She was grounded for a week longer than me. There was no way that I was going to argue with my mother. I was six, but I chose to ground myself just as long as her. I felt guilty."

"It sounds like your mother was pitting you against each other," Jett commented.

"What?" Selene was genuinely surprised by his comment. "No. Not at all. She just knew if my sister hadn't egged me on, there would be no way I would have caused trouble."

"Is that true?"

"Oh, absolutely. I mean, I'm not saying she was fully responsible, but even as kids, Astra knew her powers were more destructive than mine. So whenever she wanted to do a prank, she had me do something with my powers over water. It's easier to clean up a juice spill than a fire."

Jett blinked at her a few times as if trying to make sense of what she was saying. "I'm sorry, are you telling me that as a six-year-old, your sister could start fires?"

Selene laughed. "Yup, she sure could."

"Well, that is absolutely horrifying. I'm glad all

that little shifters can do is shift into wolves. We can track them easily enough with our own senses. But magic in a kid? Yeah, no thanks."

"That's because you don't have magic. It's not so bad. It just so happens that Bishop witches are fairly mischievous."

Jett opened his mouth to respond, but whatever he said was lost to Selene. Instead, she kept on walking.

Before her, the expansive oceanic coast spread out as far as the eye could see. It wasn't like she had never seen this sight or ones similar to it. But even so, every single time she saw it, it left her breathless. Selene had dreams of one day being able to afford a piece of land this close to the water. The fact that the Marblehead pack owned all of this was amazing to her.

This was a place she could really fall in love with. She would be able to run by the water in the morning. She would be able to take her morning coffee and cheese Danish as she watched over the ocean.

"Oh, wow, this is actually really beautiful. I hadn't realized the pack lands backed up to the ocean. It's so…" Selene wanted to repeat that the scenery itself was stunning, but it seemed that even that word wasn't descriptive enough to quantify the beauty in front of her. The ocean was out there, right in front of her, small and large waves coming to press against the beach. The small pebbles in all different shades of gray.

Selene bent down to pick up a few of them in her hands. The small rocks had been polished by the coming and going of the water over the course of time. She rubbed her fingers along the edge of a rock, over and over. Even as she rubbed the stone, she could feel it drying against her hand. The salt of the water made her skin feel sticky, but she thoroughly enjoyed being this close to the water.

It wasn't just because Selene was a water witch, though that certainly helped her feel connected to the large, rolling body of water that spread out ahead of her in shades of dark blue and white. The ocean made her feel small, but connected to the rest of the world.

"Are you okay?" Jett asked as he came to stand beside her.

"I'm fine." Her voice was soft and reverent as she kept on watching the oceanic waves move. "I love the ocean. As a witch, my affinity is water."

Jett looked out to the watery horizon, his handsome face pulled down into a deep frown. "What does that mean?" he asked.

"It means that my magic works better and is strongest when using water in spells. I'm drawn to it."

"It's nice, but I prefer the forest."

Selene snapped her neck in his direction and he gave her a shrug.

"My wolf can swim, but it's definitely not his favorite activity, if you know what I mean. He prefers running wild through the forest. We both do."

"That makes sense," she answered as she let her eyes go back to the water.

"The ocean also scares me a bit," he said.

Jett's confession made Selene take a step closer to the edge of the water.

"Why?" she asked, unable to comprehend how someone could fear the absolute beauty before them.

"It's too big. You can't see the edge of it. You can't know what kind of creatures lurk in it. At least in the forest, I know what kind of beasts I may find. I also know that I can beat all of them."

Selene cracked a smile. "Of course, that would be something you would want. You're a predator so you would never want to be in a situation where you don't know your surroundings."

"You make me sound like some kind of weak creature," he grumbled as he kicked a pebble with his shoe.

"What? Not at all. You misunderstood what I mean. Think about a lion. He's the king of the savanna, right? But if you plopped him into a frozen tundra, he wouldn't know what to do with himself. So you, as a wolf, you wouldn't want to be in a huge body of water. Your predatory skills have been honed for one setting."

Selene knew that sounded just as bad, but she found she couldn't stop talking. Maybe it was the sea air that was making her dizzy or perhaps it was Jett's proximity. He was extremely good looking, and it was hard for her to concentrate when he was beside her.

If she reached out her hand, she could touch him. She could trace the muscular shape of his forearm with her fingertips. Selene stuffed her hands in her pocket to keep herself from doing just that.

"Well, well. Look at what we have here."

"Who is this lovely lady, Jett?" the old man asked as he joined Selene and Jett on the pebbled beach.

The newcomer smiled at her warmly.

"Hey, Rick. This is Selene. She is a witch we have to keep safe for a little while."

"And here I was thinking you were showing your girlfriend around pack lands." Rick's voice was teasing.

"I don't have a girlfriend," Jett shot back as if it were common knowledge.

Selene didn't really know why, but she felt those words settle uneasily in her heart. Jett's tone had all but insinuated he wasn't relationship material. Why should that bother her so much? It shouldn't. Who was he to her? Only the wolf who had saved her from lunatic witch hunters.

But that wasn't true.

If she was being honest with herself, Selene knew her little crush on Jett could easily develop into something else. After all, he had done a lot to redeem his grumpiness. He had stopped at the grocery store to get her a cheese Danish and a sports drink. He had made her a cup of coffee after opening up his home to her.

And above all, he *had* saved her life.

He had done that because he had been ordered to do so by his alpha, but that didn't take away from the fact that he had stopped the Order of Salem from putting a bullet in her head.

Selene also couldn't quite wrap her mind around the fact that Jett had a pet bunny. A fluffy little creature that depended on him, one that Jett had saved from certain death and raised from a tiny kit.

The wolf and his rabbit.

It sounded like some kind of twisted fairy tale, but somehow, it made sense. As she watched Jett interact with Rick, she could tell Jett kept himself at a distance from other people. Hell, he had even picked a house that was far removed from the pack, the people he was meant to protect.

Selene had a feeling there was a heavy wound in his past that made Jett reluctant to trust others. He hadn't really mentioned his family, and she had a sneaking suspicion that was part of the problem.

"Selene," Rick said, taking her hand and giving it a quick peck. "What a beautiful name for such a beautiful lady. Don't let this one's permanent bad mood ruin your stay on pack lands."

"Hey," Jett quipped. "I take offense to that. I'm not always in a mad mood."

Rick raised his brows toward Selene as if he were asking her for confirmation. She giggled and immediately covered her face to try to hide the snicker. Jett shook his head, but it was with a smile on his face.

"Figures you'd charm her and gang up on me."

"You're all right, kid," Rick said. "Now, I'll leave you two. Explore, have fun. It's good to be young. I have to go on long walks just to curb the rheumatism that's started in my bones."

"I thought that shifters couldn't get sick or anything like that. Is that just a rumor?"

Jett shook his head while Rick laughed warmly.

"It's not a rumor, no," the older man answered.

"But our shifter senses tend to diminish as we age, and I'm not the young pup I used to be."

"Well, if you need company for your walks while I'm staying, feel free to come and get me." Selene smiled at him, and Rick echoed the gesture.

"She's a good one," he said as he gave Jett a pat on the shoulder.

Rick whispered something in Jett's ear that had him rolling his eyes dramatically. Selene hadn't heard what had been said, but she enjoyed seeing Jett laughing. It suited his handsome face more than any of his scowls and frowns.

For a few more minutes, Selene watched the tide. Her thoughts wandered to her sister and cousins again. She really needed to call them to make sure they were safe. Jett said they were, but he may have just been saying that to keep her calm. But then again, she trusted him.

She took in another deep breath, letting the breeze rejuvenate her. She could have stayed there for hours, but the air was getting colder and she shivered.

"We should get back to the house," Jett said as he came to stand beside her. He slipped his phone into his pocket.

"You can get phone calls this far out?" she asked.

"Coverage is spotty out here. This is a good place at the moment. I sent a text to Blaze, letting him know we are here and you're safe."

She nodded. At least Astra would know she was okay. That would have to suffice until she could get a private second to call.

He was radiating heat, and Selene took a step closer to him, feeling pulled in by the warmth.

"Any chance you can feed a witch?"

He chuckled, making her smile. "I think I can do that."

They walked back to the house, and as they did, Selene peppered Jett with questions. She wanted to know everything there was to know about shifters and how their community operated. She also had him repeat everything he knew about the Order of Salem. It wasn't much, but it was enough to know these bigoted lunatics were out for blood.

Jett led Selene into the house and gestured to the couch. "You can turn the television on while I work on lunch."

"Not on your life, wolf man. You saved my life, and I feel like I should repay the favor by making you food."

For one wild second, Selene had a dirty

thought. Maybe she could thank him in a sexier way.

"How about we both do it then," Jett responded. "A compromise."

Selene smiled at him over her shoulder as she made her way to the fridge. She swung the door opened and gasped.

"Holy meat, wolf man. Do you only ever eat cows? There's barely any veggies in there."

Jett chuckled and reach above her head and produce a head of lettuce. "I have vegetables plenty, but as you said, I'm a wolf man. I have carnivore tendencies."

"Well, just so we're clear, I'm a witch, and as a people we tend to have omnivore tastes."

"That's fair. Look in that top drawer, you'll find some peppers and cucumbers. We can cut some up and throw it on the lettuce. You know, for the omnivores." He winked at her, and her face immediately flushed.

Had she not been standing by the fridge, she might have completely melted. Who knew a wink could be so effective?

Jett took out a cutting board and while Selene chopped the veggies for her salad, he grilled four enormous burger patties.

"You know I'll barely be able to eat one of those, right? There's easily half a cow there."

He laughed, and once again, Selene felt her face flush. What was it about making this man laugh that made her giddy? She was behaving worse than a high school hornball.

"I'll be honest, three of those are for me."

Selene felt her eyes go wide and her jaw drop. "Three?"

"Yup. Shifter metabolism is crazy fast. I guess sharing our bodies with animals makes us continuously hungry."

"I have to say, I'm kind of excited to see you put those away."

"Hey, now, don't make me feel self-conscious." He nudged her playfully with his shoulder and the touched zinged energy everywhere inside her.

Yup. She had a full-blown crush. She was in deep trouble. If she didn't keep herself in check, should would find herself halfway in love with him by the time the Order of Salem was caught.

"Do you want cheese on your burger?" he asked as he dug through the fridge. He leaned over, and Selene's eyes went directly to his butt.

She had not yet known men's butts could be hot. She definitely knew now, and she wanted to take a certain song about big butts and reword it to fit Jett's own form. Selene had to bite down on her cheek from giggling.

"Hey," Jett said, stepping into her personal space. His lips were mere inches from her ear. "Just a little heads up. Shifter senses also include our smell. We can smell lies and stress, and any other kind of emotions." He gave her another wink as he pulled away.

Oh, fuck.

Her face wasn't just red and burning, it was on fire and definitely could have passed for one of the tomatoes lying on the kitchen counter.

Was he being serious? Could he smell when she was ogling him? That could only mean he had scented her rising desire for him. Selene tried not to be embarrassed, but it was impossible. She had been caught. One hundred percent caught and she didn't know how to behave anymore.

"Relax," Jett said as he flipped one of the patties in the pan. "If you were a shifter, you'd have the exact same information."

Selene couldn't breathe or swallow.

Had he just told her that he wanted her?

"Relax," Jett said as he wrangled a burger patty with the spatula. "If you were a shifter, you'd have the exact same information."

Fuck, he thought.

Yes, his wolf rejoiced, echoing the polar opposite to his own feelings.

This battle from his brain to his mouth was getting him into serious trouble.

Before today, Jett hadn't ever really thought that cooking with a woman could be that flirty and that erotically charged. But it was. And he didn't know what to do with himself. Cooking a meal with a constant hard-on was no fun, especially since he didn't want to want Selene.

There was nothing for it, though.

His wolf was pretty fucking adamant they would have her before long. It was impossible not to keep taking deep breaths. Her sweet vanilla and brown sugar scent was all that he could smell. Even if he was grilling a bunch of meat which under any other circumstance would have made his mouth water.

Now it was the woman making him feel all kinds of things.

Actually, her delectable scent wasn't the only thing tickling his nose. He could smell her desire on the air, and it was powerful. Jett didn't fully understand why she was so attracted to him. It wasn't like he was such a great catch. None of the women in the pack wanted anything to do with him. Leah was the exception because she liked to piss off her parents.

Even the mortal women he had fucked were gone by morning. That could have everything to do with his shit attitude. He hadn't exactly been as surly with Selene as he typically was.

She was seeing a side of him that only Blaze and Rick knew about. She had gotten him to tell her the full Bugsy story, and he hadn't stopped being worried for her wellbeing since she had passed out in the cafe.

The fact that she was his mate weighed heavily on him. That was why he kept wanting her to be happy and content in his home. That was why he had gotten all up in her space. Well, that and because he had wanted to touch her. His fingers had all but reached out to touch the soft blonde waves of her hair.

Do it, his wolf demanded. *We'll get there eventually. Stop fighting it.*

Jett didn't know if other shifters had ever fought the mate sense. He had a feeling it was something that was easier said than done. Even now, he was imagining what it would be like to lead Selene back to his bed. He could have her for lunch instead of the burgers. He would lick her sweet center, drinking in all of her juices until she came on his tongue.

Can't fight this. She's our mate. Do it.

Jett tried to focus all of his energy into cooking, but it was difficult. He kept on catching himself watching Selene as if looking at her preparing a salad was the most entertainment he'd had in decades.

"It's ready," he finally announced. His voice sounded rough even to his ears.

How he would manage to keep up the fight against his mating instincts was beyond him. But he would have to do it, though. If he just kept repeating it to himself, maybe he could drown out the sound of his wolf howling for Selene.

Jett plated one patty on a fresh bun and handed it to her. Their fingers grazed, and he could have sworn he felt a zing of electricity pass between them. As if something had been turned on, something had begun.

"Thanks." She took the plate from his hands, but she didn't move. Jett could only hope she had also felt the surge of energy between them.

Selene's heart was beating so fast, he could hear it jumping erratically in her chest. Her breath was making her breasts move up and down in an alluring rhythm. He knew she wanted him. Her entire body was alive with it.

Jett felt himself leaning down before he even really knew what he was doing. His lips grazed hers softly and her sharp inhale of breath pulled him from his momentarily lapse of sanity. He pulled away and cleared his throat.

"Shit. Sorry."

"No," she whispered, her voice heavy and breathy. "Don't." She stood on the tips of her toes and placed her soft lips against his in a sweet, quick kiss.

She pulled away slowly, almost as if she were debating about taking another shot at his mouth. She licked her lips, and he mimicked the gesture, tasting her on his tongue. She tasted just like she smelled, vanilla and brown sugar. Jett was suddenly very desperate to know if her pussy would taste just as delicious.

Selene took a few steps back, in a daze. She set her plate on the counter and grabbed her fork to push her salad around. Jett took a seat in front of her and watched her through his lowered eyes. Needing a distraction for what had just happened, he took one of his burgers, drenched it with ketchup and took a bite.

He hadn't realized that Selene was watching him. Her blue eyes were wide.

"I can totally see how you would eat three of those burgers. You just shoved half of one into your mouth. That was impressive."

"It's the only way to enjoy it," he said after swallowing.

"By stuffing your face?"

"Don't knock it 'til you've tried it," he teased.

Selene eyed the burger and she brought it to her mouth. Jett was fascinated as she took a large bite. He was trying very hard not to imagine a different kind of meat going into her mouth. She was having a difficult time chewing and her face was red, no doubt from having his eyes on her.

When she finally swallowed, she coughed and shook her head.

"Okay, no. I am not doing that again and I really don't know why you say it's more enjoyable that way."

Jett shrugged. "That might be a shifter thing."

"Now he tells me," she scoffed, but there was a smile on her face.

"I also could have been teasing you a bit," he admitted.

"Of course. And I fell for it." Her laughter was light and warm. It made his wolf happy.

This was nice. He had to admit. He hadn't ever had a woman in his house sharing a meal they had prepared together. Actually, he couldn't even remember the last time he had cooked for anyone but himself. It was kind of wonderful having her in his place, joking around and chatting as they ate.

This must be what his alpha was always going

on about. This had to be what Blaze was missing in his life. The intimacy of sharing small, mundane, everyday things.

Jett had never had them to begin with. Not when his mother was around, and definitely not after she left. This was the first real taste of companionable domesticity he ever had, and he was enjoying it. He ignored his wolf howling in victory.

Being comfortable and at ease with Selene in his space didn't mean he would let such a wonderful woman align herself with the likes of him. But he would have her in his space for a little while. That would have to be enough to hold him for the rest of his life once she was gone.

"Do you think we can call Astra once we're done eating?"

"Of course," he answered. He wasn't trying to keep her away from her family, he just didn't understand what it was like to miss someone. To worry about someone.

Jett did worry about the safety of the pack and the security of its people, but having someone to feel disconnected from wasn't something he was used to.

They continued to eat their meal, but Jett was

feeling introspective, and didn't engage Selene into much of a conversation. Once she was done, she took her plate to the sink and began cleaning up.

"You don't have to do that," he instructed.

"Sure I do. You've opened your home to me, and you fed me. That means I get to do the cleanup."

Jett took his plate to the sink and put the condiments and other ingredients into their places.

Selene dunked her hands into the water and she scrubbed at some dishes. She was swaying as she worked. Jett let his eyes go to her hips. He even went so far as to imagine what it would feel like to grip those luscious curves in his hands and sway along with her.

Inspired by the dirty images in his head, he took out his phone and connected the device to his speaker. He picked a playlist and the music began to softly stream through the kitchen.

"Good call," Selene gave him a smile from over her shoulder. "I always have music playing at the house when I do chores."

"Let me know if the genre isn't to your liking," he said.

But Selene shook her head. "Music is music. So long as I can shake my booty to it, I like it."

Jett was fond of that attitude. His appreciation for Selene's beliefs about music only increased when a particularly upbeat song came onto the speaker and she started shaking her ass. He licked his lips, feeling his erection strain against his pants. He was about ready to burst out of his jeans. From over her shoulder, Selene gave him a smile, and he all but lost it. He doubted she would appreciate it if he decided to cop a feel.

"Don't you ever let loose? Come on, wolf man. Shake those hips."

Selene's hands were still in the sudsy sink, but she stopped what she was doing to wait for him to move. With a shake of his head, Jett sighed. "I don't really know how to dance." The admission shouldn't have embarrassed him, but it did.

Selene dried her hands with a towel and came to stand in front of him. When she placed her hands on his hips, his cock screamed at him for attention.

"Move with the music." She giggled as she tried to get him to move with her.

Jett was very aware if she got any close to him, she would feel his erection. He was sure she wouldn't appreciate it. But she wasn't relenting, so he grabbed a hold of her hips, and keeping a foot of distance between them, he started to sway along with her. It was heaven and painful torture all at once.

Jett didn't want to let her go. Especially not when she was giving him that beautiful smile. He decided he could stay like that forever. Just moving to the beat of the music with Selene *right* there. His wolf was almost mad with lust, and so was he.

The song was interrupted by a ringing. Jett cursed under his breath and he rushed forward. That was Blaze's ringtone. He quickly unhooked the phone from the speaker and shoved the device up to his ear.

The interruption hadn't exactly been ideal, and Jett was frustrated. Couldn't a wolf catch a break for one second?

"Alpha, hey," he mumbled into the phone.

"Jett, I got your texts. I'm pleased that you're safe now. Put Selene on. Let the sisters talk for a bit."

He placed a hand on the phone's speaker and gestured Selene over with a nod. "Come speak with you sister real quick."

Selene's bright smile got even sunnier. She took the phone from his hand.

"Astra?" Selene asked.

"Selene, hey," her twin responded. "How are you?"

Jett wanted to feel bad for being able to eavesdrop with his shifter hearing, but he was kind of hoping the conversation between the two sisters would yield some kind of information for him.

"I've had the weirdest day," his mate said, shooting him a grin.

"Tell me about it." Astra agreed before giving her twin a fairly detailed account of her own day. Apparently, a certain Mrs. Gellar was involved, and Astra had called it. Selene's cheeks were red, and Jett could smell the sorrow on her.

"Shit, I'm sorry. Do you think it would have made a difference if we had caught on earlier to the fact she is an evil witch hunter?"

"Honestly?" Astra said over the phone. "No. I think it would have put us in more danger. At least now we have the wolves on our side. That's something our witchy ancestors didn't have in 1692. It might just save us so history doesn't repeat itself."

Selene's eyes were on his, and there was a slight

furrow to her brow. Jett couldn't decipher the emotion there.

"That's a very valid point. Hey, Astra? Fate is strong, right?"

There was a pause on the call. Jett also needed a pause. Why was Selene asking her twin about fate? His wolf was bounding around in his mind, convinced their mate was feeling things for Jett.

"Yes, but why?" Astra asked. "Why are you asking me that? Is everything okay?"

"Yeah, it is. It's fine." Selene was still looking at him. "I've got to go. Be safe, okay? And try to convince your wolf to call mine tomorrow. I think my guy needs to be called so I can get any sort of information. He's surly." She winked at him with a crooked smile.

She was full on teasing him. It made him want to play. Dirty little naked games.

"Surly? Hey, Selene? You know that guy in that show we watch? The one with all of those people trying to get the throne?"

"That fantasy one with the dire wolves? The one that has you obsessed because of that one actor?"

"Uh-huh. Yup. That one." There was silence on the other line. Selene shrugged at him.

"Why do I feel like you're speaking in code?" Selene asked.

"That actor? He's got a doppelganger."

"Huh?" Selene asked, then her eyes sparkled. Her grin widened to a full-on smile that made Jett's heart skip a few beats. "Oh. Ooh. Wow. Cool. Well, have fun. Talk tomorrow."

She ended the call and place it onto the counter. Selene was suddenly closing her arms around his neck, her lips going to his. She kissed him, her tongue taking a taste of the inside of his mouth.

Jett was so shocked, he didn't move.

Selene had just kissed him.

CHAPTER ELEVEN

SELENE

Selene's head was finally catching up to her actions. She didn't even feel any of the steps she took. Nor did she even realize what she was doing until her mouth was firmly planted onto Jett's. Her tongue dipped into his mouth and her arms went around his neck.

She only realized what she was doing when her toes curled because *boy, oh boy*, Jett could kiss. And he was doing it like he had been made to love her mouth. He knew just how much tongue to slip, he knew just the right kind of pressure to press to her lips. When his hands cupped her ass and squeezed, Selene felt herself melt a little. A lot, actually.

If they could just keep kissing forever, she would be very happy.

"Selene?" Jett asked against her lips, and she immediately pushed back from him. So much for being the rebellious twin.

"Sorry," she mumbled, feeling her face flush. "I don't know what came over me."

Jett cleared his throat and rubbed a hand on his short-cropped hair. "It's okay, really. I just wasn't expecting that."

"Neither was I, to be honest." Selene's embarrassment was made all the more real with *that* particular confession. She didn't need to tell him that.

"I just don't want there to be any confusion," Jett said with a pained voice. "I don't have the best reputation when it comes to women, and I don't want you to do anything you'd regret."

Selene waited a few more seconds before he explained what kind of reputation he had, but Jett didn't say anything more. She licked her lips, and the taste of their kiss was still there. She tried to commit the feeling of it to memory. Selene had never been kissed like that. No single kiss had ever made her feel so completely dizzy with want. She watched Jett, waiting for him to speak, but he said nothing, averting his eyes.

"Care to explain what you mean by reputation?

Joan Jett kind of reputation?" she added that musical reference in hopes to lighten the mood.

Jett's laugh was small and it wasn't as sincere as she would have hoped. "Something like that. I sleep around, Selene. I'm not a good man."

Selene swallowed the bile that was suddenly rising in the back of her throat.

Of course, the first man she would choose to kiss in years would turn out being some kind of fuck boy. She crossed her arms as she tried to figure out what to do. She didn't really know Jett, but if she was honest with herself, she kind of liked him.

He was a sweet man, and though he was abrasive at first, Selene knew he had a good heart. He was funny and kind. Could fuck boys be all of those things? Selene didn't know. She didn't know enough about all of that stuff to make up her mind.

"I'm not the relationship type, you know?" Jett added. "And you're a special woman. You're too..." he stopped himself. "We should keep this platonic."

"Okay," she said.

"Not that I didn't enjoy the kiss," he said, his eyes meeting hers. "It was a good kiss, but...well, you should keep those kisses for a better man."

"It was just a kiss," Selene said. It took every

effort to shrug and roll her eyes like it wasn't a big deal. Like she went around kissing men all the time.

She didn't, obviously. But it was suddenly very clear to her that maybe she had been living the life of a recluse a bit too well if she went around kissing men she barely knew. She could try to explain it away and blame it on the fact that he had saved her, and that was a big deal. She knew on a deeper level it was more than that. She was definitely attracted to Jett Arrowood.

Selene stepped away from the kitchen. She wasn't embarrassed by Jett's rebuttal, but she also didn't want to linger in the kitchen, close to him and his delicious looking lips.

"So," she shrugged, "what are we supposed to do to pass the time?" she asked.

She knew what her body wanted to do, but she didn't know if it would be all that cautious to fall into bed with Jett. Not only had he said he wanted to keep things platonic, but she also didn't know how long she would be holed up in his house. If the sex was bad, it would be awkward to stay with him. Not that Selene believed it would be bad. If Jett's kissing skills were any indications to his skills in the bedroom, she wouldn't need to fear mediocre sex.

"We could watch television," he suggested. "Maybe go for another walk along the beach, or if you prefer, we can play a game."

"A game?" Selene's interest perked right up. She adored all kinds of board games. "What kind of game?"

Jett opened a small cupboard beneath the television stand and took out a few board games. Selene immediately spotted Uno, a game she loved to play, and one she always beat Astra in. Selene was the Uno champion of the Bishop family. She might love board games, but card games were her specialty.

She reached out and grabbed the pack of cards. Taking them to kitchen table, she was already shuffling the cards. "Let's play this," she said as she settled into a chair. She was giggling like a little girl because she knew there was no chance in hell he could beat her.

Jett sat in the seat in front of her and he held out his hands for the cards. "Why don't I shuffle those?"

She slapped the cards to her chest, away from his outstretched palm. "Why?"

"Because you're sitting there, grinning like a fool. So either you're already cheating, or you need to get out more. No one loves playing Uno this much."

Selene laughed because he wasn't wrong. She would never cheat at a game; she had way too much integrity for that. But there was truth in what he said about not getting out much.

"I run a holistic health center, which basically means I am a small business owner. Do you know how many hours a day I work? Not just with clients, but doing the administrative stuff?"

Jett shook his head, but he leaned in. Selene took it as a sign he was actually interested in what she was saying.

"I get to the center at seven, even if we open at nine. I do all kinds of stuff, like make sure the rooms are clean and ready to go. I go over the day's appointments and send out reminders, either by email or phone calls, to upcoming clients. I do the accounting, restock our supplies of towels and it just goes on and on."

"Doesn't your sister help?"

"She does more client work than me," Selene said with a shrug. "She's a Reiki master. I'm not. I don't have the same affinity for energy as she does. Which really annoys me, but we all have our strengths. I'm the brains of the organization, I guess."

"I get it," Jett said as he looked down at the cards Selene had drawn out for him. "Blaze owns the only shifter bar for miles around. I work there with him. I'm the barback, the security team, and bartender all rolled into one. It's long hours, especially since we don't close until one or two in the morning."

Selene felt her eyes go wide in surprise. "Ew. That's way too late for me. I'm in bed at nine."

"Yes, but what time do you wake up?" he asked with a light chuckle.

"Around five. So by the time I'm getting up, you're just going to bed."

That meant they had completely different schedules. Another great reason not to be affected by his hot bod, warm eyes, and delicious kisses.

The went on to play a few rounds of Uno, all the while chatting about everything and nothing. Selene beat him with every hand, but that wasn't what was giving her the rush. It wasn't winning hand after hand that made her giddy.

It was Jett.

There was an easiness between them. Conversation just flowed, and laughter seemed to be a guarantee.

"All of this losing has made me hungry," Jett mumbled as he pushed away from the table.

"Oh?" Selene giggled, watching Jett stomp off into the kitchen.

He pulled open a cabinet door and took out a bag of marshmallows and a box of puffed rice cereal.

"What are you doing?" she asked, standing by the counter.

"I'm going to make squares," he answered nonchalantly.

"Are you in the habit of making your own snacks?" This was more of a wonderment, one she very well could have kept to herself, but the words flew out.

Jett chuckled as he went on, mixing the ingredients in a large glass bowl. "Yes, absolutely." There was a silence for a little while as she watched him work. "When I was a kid," he said, "a lot of the other kids had moms that made them snacks and baked all kinds of cool things. I didn't have that, so I started making my own. I could only do simple things, but…" The *ding* of the microwave nearly made Selene jump. She wanted to hear the rest of his thought.

Whatever Jett had been about to say, he didn't feel the need to continue. He pressed down the cereal and marshmallow mixture into a pan and set it aside. He took a small packet of chocolate chips and nuked them.

"What are you doing?" she asked.

"Well, I have a guest. I have to make the fancy kind of squares."

Selene's brow furrowed. It wasn't until he was drizzling the melted chocolate onto the setting puffed rice that she understood. She was fascinated, watching him drizzle the chocolate into a fancy pattern.

Shit, this man was more intriguing than any cooking show Selene could have watched.

Jett tucked the pan into the fridge before turning to wink at her. "It'll be ready in a few minutes. Want a glass of milk with your squares?"

All she could do was nod. How was this the grumpy man who had snapped at Lester in the cafe? Selene supposed that hadn't really been him. This version of Jett she was seeing was the real one. The one who cared for a guest like his life depended on it.

"So tell me. How often do you need to eat to keep from passing out?"

Selene's brain had to catch up to the question. "It depends on how I feel, how much moving around I'm doing."

"Are you diabetic or something?" he seemed genuinely interested, so Selene licked her suddenly very dry lips.

"No. I have low-blood sugar. It's called hypo-glycemia, but I'm not diabetic. It's just this thing I have. The doctors were baffled by it when I was a kid. It just seems to be a stress response my body has."

"Cool. Well, this should help." He took the pan out of the fridge and proceeded to cut a few squares out. He placed one on a plate and nudged it toward her.

"Were you really hungry, or did you just get worried that I would pass out on you?"

Jett blushed. He actually *blushed*. It made him look sweet, not just insanely hot. It was a dangerous mixture on Selene's nervous system.

"Sort of. I mean, don't get me wrong. Shifters are *always* hungry, but I was also a bit worried."

Selene had to keep all of her focus on the square on her plate. She brought it to her mouth and took a bite, enjoying the added taste of the chocolate on her tongue. Her heart was doing this weird thing, and she knew.

She was in serious trouble.

CHAPTER TWELVE

JETT

J ett watched intently as Selene brought the snack to those beautiful lips of hers. He had to swallow a few times to keep his wolf from completely tearing out of him to get to Selene. Watching her eat was quickly becoming one of his favorite things because it brought attention to her mouth. It also made him feel good to know he was taking care of her.

That's because she's our mate. We should *be taking care of her.*

His animal was having all kinds of fantasies about the different kinds of things he could feed her. There was a box of freezy pops in the freezer that was all but calling his name. But Jett knew that watching Selene suck on one of those would kill him. He had to readjust the situation growing in his pants as he grabbed one square and bit into it to keep from kissing Selene.

The doorbell rang, and he saw his mate startle.

"Don't worry," he reassured her. "It's probably one of the pack members looking for Blaze."

He made his way to the front door to see Rick standing there. Seeing the man twice in only a few short hours was uncommon. "Is everything okay?" he asked, stepping out onto the small porch.

Rick nodded and took a seat in one of the stairs. "Have you spoken to Blaze recently?"

Jett nodded. "We've been keeping track of each other since we had to rescue those Salem witches."

"Did he tell you the witch he saved, Astra, she's his mate?"

His mouth was dry and he tried to clear his throat against the emotions this new information birthed inside him. Jett couldn't believe it. How did that even happen? What were the chances that he and the alpha each saved a witch from certain death to discover they had rescued their mates?

Slim to fucking none.

And yet, that's exactly what was happening.

Jett sighed and rubbed a hand across his short hair. Wolves didn't really get aches and pains, but he was sure he was about to have one major headache. He cleared his throat and shook his head. "Blaze must be happy to have finally found was he's been looking for all these years."

"Oh, he's happier than a pig in shit. She's a sweet lady, too. He's lucky."

Jett nodded because he didn't know what else to do. Rick was an old wolf, and one of the only pack elders who actually respected Jett. The old wolf had never been one of those who gossiped about Jett and his family. He had also not discouraged the friendship between Blaze and Jett like the others had. All of this meant that Jett didn't mind Rick so much. He was like a stand-in father in a lot of ways.

"Are you going to get to the point you're trying to make?" he asked Rick.

The old man chuckled and shook his head. "I sure am. I have a feeling that your own witch is important to you. Am I wrong?"

Jett didn't answer. He didn't want to. He was still battling with this wolf about Selene and what she did or did not mean for them.

"Your silence says everything you don't want to, kid. She's yours, isn't she? She's your mate." Rick hadn't phrased it as a question.

How the old man had been able to deduce that was beyond Jett. That went way over what shifter senses could do. It must have been some wisdom mixed in with a lucky guess.

"What are you going to do about it?" Rick asked. But he barely gave Jett any time to answer. "Because I know exactly what you *should* do. Do you hear me, Jett? You've found your mate, and fate was kind enough to bring her in a way that means she's stuck with your stubborn ass for the foreseeable future.

"You should use this time to play nice. Seduce her, however you kids do that these days. If it wasn't for these witch hunters playing god, you wouldn't have a chance of making that woman stick around your gruff ass for more than ten seconds."

"I don't want a mate," Jett said. It made him ache to say that. His wolf was huffing and puffing. "Never asked for one. Never needed one. That's Blaze's dream. Not mine."

"Oh?" Rick asked. "And what is it that you've always wanted, Jett? Acceptance? A place to belong? People of your own? What do you think a mate is?"

Jett's jaw was clenched so hard, it made his

temples aches. He didn't want to answer these questions. He didn't feel ready to even think about all of this mate business. Just that day, he had woken with a failed booty call in his bed. That didn't make him prime mate material. Jett might not have known Selene for a long time, but he knew she deserved a hell of a lot more than what he would be able to give her.

Rick might say that having a mate meant acceptance, that it meant having someone all his own, but Jett wasn't so sure that wolves like him where meant for that kind of happiness.

"Look, kid. She's here. She's in your life. Don't fight it. You'll only hurt yourself, and you don't deserve that." Rick pushed off the step and stood directly in Jett's line of sight. "You already feel connected to her. It shows. Your entire demeanor is softer. Even your shoulders have relaxed a bit."

Jett grunted his response, but mostly because he didn't know what else to say.

"Be good," Rick said. The old wolf walked down the path, whistling a tune.

Jett watched him go, frozen in place. His head was full of all kinds of things. Was Rick right? Should he really lean into the mate thing? *Yes*, his wolf insisted. Was he even worthy of a good woman like Selene? *Yes,* he wolf howled, *and if you don't feel like you are, then earn it. Mate. She is our mate.*

He ran a hand across the back of his neck. This was a lot. Jett let his mind wander. He tried to imagine mating Selene. He pictured what it would be like to have a life with her. Shit, he even had a very vivid picture of a couple of kids running around. That made him shiver.

Jett knew nothing about being a father. One of the reasons why he didn't want to be mated was because he truly feared becoming like his father. There was no way in hell he was going to put more kids through neglect and abandonment.

"Are you okay?" Selene's soft voice came from behind him, making him jump. Fuck. He had been so engrossed in his thoughts, his shifter senses hadn't even alerted him to the fact she was behind him.

"Yup. Yes. Fine." He blew out a breath. That had been one too many words in one second.

Jett had no time to recover.

"What are mates?" Selene asked.

"What are mates?" Selene repeated after a few seconds had passed. Her arms were crossed, but she dropped them and cocked her head to the side as if she were assessing him.

Jett bristled. How in the fuck did she know about mates? Had she heard every word from his conversation with Rick? That was pretty fucking horrible. He hated the aching feeling that knowledge elicited. He didn't like this kind of attention. He shook his head and walked past her to get to his kitchen. Throwing open the fridge door, he grabbed a beer and twisted off the cap before flicking it onto the kitchen counter.

Selene followed him into the kitchen and did

the same. She took a swing of the beer and immediately pulled a face.

"Ew, this stuff is nasty."

She shook her head with her cute little pink tongue sticking out of her mouth. Jett chuckled despite himself. Just seeing her there in his house being her naturally adorable self was enough to make him feel at ease. Rick's words about his tense shoulders popped into his head. *Well, shit.*

"It's not, though, " he said, taking another long pull from his own bottle.

"It's gross. Now tell me what mates are. Because I accidentally heard part of your conversation with that nice man, Rick."

Jett shook his head. "It's nothing. Just a shifter thing."

"Explain for the witch, please."

He took a deep breath and blew it out slowly. There was no way in hell Selene was going to let this go.

"Fine. So shifters have insanely good reflexes, and we have all of these senses. One of those is the mate sense. The animal senses our mates, and when we find those people, it's hard to ignore the call. Or the pull, or whatever you want to call it."

"Does this happen a lot? Like do you often meet women your wolf calls out mate for?"

He shook his head again. He was doing a shit job at explaining this. "No. It only happens once. My wolf told me when I found my mate. My soul mate."

Selene's cheeks reddened and she looked away from him. He didn't miss the way she took a tiny step away from him.

"Your soul mate. Your wolf tells you who you're meant to be with for the rest of your life?"

"Yes," he grinded out. It hurt to talk about this with her.

"Okay." She drew out the word with her cheeks going a deep shade of red. "And your wolf said that I'm your mate."

He nodded. "But it doesn't mean anything, all right? I mean, we're strangers. You don't know me and I don't know you. If you knew more about me, you would know that I'm a bad bet to make. We'll just pretend this never happened."

"But," her brow furrowed, "what happens to a wolf if he doesn't get the mate he's met? Does it kill the animal inside you?"

Perceptive little witch.

Of course, she would guess that ignoring the

mate call would hurt. It wouldn't kill Jett or the beast inside of him right away. But it sure would hurt like a mother fucker to ignore. Every day, a bigger part of him would die until he actually died.

Good thing I'm already heartless, he told himself. His wolf was thrashing inside his mind, demanding to be let out. Jett knew if the wolf were to take control, the animal would bite Selene to force him into matehood. That's not what he wanted.

Not for Selene.

She was too sweet, too kind for him. He would repeat that until his wolf believed the words. That's what was best. Right?

The image of a pregnant Selene holding a little girl that looked just like her flashed through his mind. How did he get *that* without hurting Selene? Was that even possible?

"Jett?" his name on her lips did something to his heart and he commanded the organ to behave.

"It doesn't feel too good, but it's fine," he answered.

"I'm causing you pain?" she asked on a whisper.

"No, fuck. Selene, I'm not good with words. I can't explain this properly."

She gave him an encouraging smile. "You're doing just fine."

He could smell her confusion, and it damn near broke his heart. He didn't even want to know what she must think of him.

"I have an idea." She snapped her fingers and her smile brightened. "You don't want to be mates, right? Because we're strangers and all that." That wasn't it, but Jett wasn't going to correct her. "So what if we're just mates who are friends? Would that work?"

Jett clenched his teeth. How did he tell her that the mating wasn't complete until he fucked her? That it wouldn't be real until he bit her while he was coming deep inside her.

Despite himself, Jett imagined just what it would be like to do just that. He didn't like how much he enjoyed the naughty images playing through his head.

"Friends?" he managed to ask with a suddenly very dry throat. "You want to be friends?"

"Well, if we're meant to be, we can start as friends."

Jett was watching her closely, and she met his gaze, almost daring him to say no. He took a deep breath, letting her sweet scent fill his nostrils. He could be her friend. They could be close. At least for a while. Then she would wise up and leave just like everyone else did. Or maybe, he would be the one to bail first. To protect himself. That was normal for him.

"What do you say, wolf man? Friends?" She held out her hand for him to shake.

He took her small one into his and he immediately felt that surge of energy he always did when she had her hands on him.

"Yup. Sounds good."

He tried to give her a smile, but it felt forced. He hoped she wouldn't notice.

"Now, sit your butt back down. I want to beat you at Crazy Eights."

Jett's eyes tracked her as she grabbed a pack of cards from his cupboard and settled into her seat.

She didn't know, but she'd beaten him already. Not at Crazy Eights. Nope. She'd beaten down some of his defenses. Jett sat across from her and took his cards, knowing it was a lost cause.

CHAPTER FOURTEEN

SELENE

S pending the day with Jett had been an interesting experience. He was much nicer and sweeter than he gave himself credit for, but she also felt a deep darkness within him, a deep pain. Selene couldn't believe she was actually managing to enjoy herself even if she was technically in hiding in the Marblehead pack lands.

By all rights, she should have been freaking the fuck out and on a tear to get to her twin and cousins. They needed to make sure the Order of Salem didn't hurt any witches, whether they were related to them or not. But Selene also had enough good sense to know four witches against people with guns was not a good idea.

It definitely didn't help that their magic drained

out fairly quickly, and they had never been taught offensive magic. That wasn't needed in everyday life. It hadn't really been taught to any of the witches in Salem in the last few generations. It was like somehow, the horrors of the witch trials had faded into a distant memory. Like it had been nothing but a nasty nightmare.

Selene had never expected to want offensive magic. There had never been any situation in her life that would have warranted it. This attack by the witch hunters had come out of left field.

Had she been silly and naive to believe she was lucky enough to live in a safer world than her ancestors?

"Whoa, there." Jett waved a hand in her face from across the table. "Are you okay? You just got really quiet all of a sudden."

Selene shook her head, trying to clear her mind. "Yes, I'm fine. I just... You know what? It's nothing. Never mind."

"I won't press you, but if you want to talk..." He looked around the small dining room. "There's no one here but me. Unload. Tell me what's on your mind."

With a sigh, she dropped her cards down and leaned onto the table, framing her face with her hands. "I'm just concerned about my family. About all of the witches out there who don't have a wolf pack to protect them."

"We have the entire witch communities of Salem and Marblehead covered." Jett stood and took the seat beside her. "It's going to be okay."

"I mean, sure. That's nice. But it makes me ache for my ancestors. I don't get it. Why does the world hate us just because we have a different set of skills than they do? Rebecca Bishop, my ancestor, she was a great healer. She was actually a very respected and needed member of the community. They turned on her so quickly."

"That won't happen this time around." Jett's tone was pitched low, like he was making a promise.

"How do you know?" she whispered, feeling a little bit sad.

"Because I won't let anything happen to you."

Now *that* didn't sound like a promise. It was something heavier.

"Is that a mate thing?" she felt compelled to ask by the darkening of his eyes.

"Yes." His voice was breathy and powerful, all at once. The sound of it made Selene shiver.

Jett was just *that* good. He could make her feel

all kinds of things with one word. She held her breath, wondering what to do next. She wanted to kiss him, but that hadn't turned out so well for her earlier. She felt a little wild. Like she should kiss him again. Like this time, he would let her. Like this time, it would lead to more.

So much more. Selene wanted that. She wanted to know what it would be like to press herself close to him. To feel her naked breasts against him. Selene clenched her core, hoping to dampen her sudden need to jump on Jett.

"Selene?" he asked, his voice still low and his eyes still dark.

Before she could even say anything else, he was standing and going to the kitchen, his steps long and purposeful.

"Please tell me you like steak," he said, swinging the fridge door with so much force, she was sure it would come off its hinges.

His sudden shift in mood made Selene wonder if shifters could also alter their moods. She was too confused. She was positive they had been on the brink of sharing a moment, but instead of leaning into it, like she was ready to do, he had fully walked away.

To talk about meat.

By god, did this man spend every waking hour just thinking about his next meal? The puffed rice squares were still churning away in her stomach, *and* she had low-blood sugar. Maybe Jett needed medical attention.

Or maybe, *just* maybe, he was using cooking food as a way to distract himself from the connection that sparked between them. Selene wasn't crazy. She knew it was there. It would have been pretty great if Jett could see it, too. She had a feeling it wasn't enough for mates to be friends. After all, *mate* was another term for fucking. Selene thought maybe Jett was purposefully distancing himself from her. She wasn't about to give into any thoughts that it was because he wasn't attracted to her.

Sure, she was on the curvy side, but she wore those like nobody's business. And the way he looked at her, like she was a juicy steak, was all she needed to know there was something to this mate thing.

"Do you like steak?" Jett repeated the question as he rifled through his fully stocked fridge.

Selene watched him closely, looking for any sign that his resolve was wavering. That he would turn around, lift her onto the kitchen counter and make a meal out of *her*. Oh, wow. What was with her? Jett had managed to turn her into a sex-craved woman with only a couple of kisses.

"What would you do if I said no?" she asked to see what his answer would be. She was also teasing him, hoping to keep the tension between them alive and well.

"I don't know, offer you something else. But I'm a wolf shifter. I need my meat."

"I'm just messing with you." She sighed. He wasn't biting on the playful banter. *Damn.* "I love steak, so long as it doesn't bleed on my plate."

"Oh, man," he shook his head, "that's the best part. A nice rare steak is my favorite."

"Yikes." Selene was almost gagging at the thought of a barely cooked steak. "I'm going to need mine to be more on the well-done side."

Jett turned to face her, his mouth wide open. "That is seriously messing with the integrity of the cut. It burns away all of the most delicious things about steak."

"Well, can I ask you something then? Do you like your steak rare because it pleases the wolf inside of you?" There it was, that spark was back. *Fan it, lady. You've got this.*

"Huh," Jett answered. "I hadn't thought of it that way. But he sure likes it."

Well, shit. Flirting was a hell of a lot more complicated to do when she was trying to be all covert about it. Her lack of skills was seriously bugging her.

"Right," she said, floundering. "And do you eat animals when you're in your wolf shape?"

Selene wasn't too comfortable with knowing the answer. She didn't want to imagine Jett as a wolf eating a rabbit. What if he accidentally ate Bugsy one day? Yup. This was all out sexy talk.

"I mean, I do eat animals in my wolf shape. That hunt of a prey is half the fun. But I don't eat rabbit anymore. I have a hard time looking at those furry creatures and not thinking of Bugsy."

She couldn't resist her smile. It was like Jett had read her mind. More than that, he also made sure not to eat his pet's kin. That was kind of sweet. Jett liked to pretend that he was this big, badass wolf who wasn't emotional, who didn't need anyone but himself, but with only one day with him, Selene was already starting to see beyond that.

He was the sweet man who had rescued her. He had even brought her a cheese Danish when she had been on the verge of passing out. He remembered little things and that spoke to a kind nature. He made treats while playing cards and drizzled chocolate in fancy patterns.

He was a man with many different layers, a lot of them soft and gooey like the melted chocolate. Though Selene suspected he had to keep that away from the other wolves. As enforcer, he probably had a specific image he wanted to portray. That didn't include baking, probably.

She liked to think he only did that for her.

CHAPTER FIFTEEN

SELENE

Selene and Jett cooked dinner, working in tandem again. While he manned the grill, because the man had an actual grill top on his stove, Selene took care of the sides. As she cut up potatoes and turnips, she did everything she could to brush up against him. She didn't miss that he always leaned into the touch before moving away. He even mumbled to himself a few times. She could only catch a few words, but it had mostly been *nuts*, and *hard*, and *mate*. She could only hope that the rest of those sentences were the dirty kind.

"This is ready," he said, pointing to her steak. The other one, which was much larger, was still uncooked.

She gave him a pointed look, but he smiled and gave her a wink. "By the time we get the sides onto our plates, that will be ready."

Selene didn't even try to stop her shudder. "That's practically still mooing." She gasped.

Jett chuckled, his hand going to her waist. "Hardly," he said as he moved around her.

The touch was light, but it was enough to make her entire body sing. Selene had to distract herself by stirring the vegetables frying in a pan. She dished some onto two plates, acutely aware that Jett was standing very close to her.

"Are you making sure I do this right?" she teased.

"Yup." He laughed. "I sure am."

A few moments later, when the steaks were cooked—basically raw for him and nice and charred for her—they sat down to eat. Again.

"I feel like all we do is eat," she mused, taking a sip of water.

"It's a shifter thing. Sorry. I figured you'd get it because of the low-blood sugar thing."

"Right. I guess I do. It runs in my dad's family, like I said. But my twin didn't get it. Good thing I'm the responsible one. I can't imagine what would have happened to Astra if she had to keep track of what she eats. She's wonderful, but she's a little bit of a scatterbrain."

"So you two are very close, right?"

"Oh, yeah. The closest. But it's not just us two. Our cousins Raven and Cerise are practically sisters to us."

"You have some very interesting names in your family," he mused.

"You think so, Jett? Where does that name come from, anyway?"

He ran a hand across the back of his neck and sighed. She hadn't meant to touch a nerve, but she definitely had.

"It was my mom's idea. I never got a chance to ask her why she picked that, of all things."

"I'm so sorry. I didn't realize something had happened to her."

Jett laughed dryly. "Something happened to her, all right."

Selene was just about to ask for more details, but at the very last second, she thought better of it. Maybe if she stayed silent, Jett would choose to say something.

"She bailed when I was three," he finally continued. The words looked painful to say. "I haven't seen her since. If I did, I wouldn't even know her."

Once again, silence reigned between them, and Selene had to wonder if this was because she was willing to just listen. She was fine with letting the silence get long and drawn out. She had to wonder if anyone had ever just given him the chance to speak. Or maybe the wolves in the pack had always felt compelled to ignore him, or to explain his parents' behaviors away. Regardless, Selene was fine with being the person Jett confided to.

"It was just my dad and me for a little while. He wasn't really a favored membered of the pack. He was a lot of trouble. He fought with the elders all the time. We lived in a small shack in the woods just on the outskirts of pack lands because of that. It was better for everyone to keep him away from the others. He would start fights if he saw another living soul."

Selene swallowed hard at those last words. They seemed to mean so much more than what he had said. It made her sad to think about what Jett could have been through at the hands of his own father.

"I'm sorry," she whispered. Because what else could she say?

"My dad was an alcoholic," Jett said with a shrug as if that explained away everything. "That isn't something that's easy to be when you're a shifter. We have insane metabolisms and we process alcohol really fast. He would drink bottles of hard liquor like they were beer. He always found a way to be drunk. One night, he drank way too much and got into a fight. He killed two people before they were able to subdue him. He's going to be in prison for a very long time."

Now that she had heard all of Jett's history, his reluctance at having a mate and his general attitude made a lot of sense. His past actually explained a lot of his behavior. In a lot of ways, he was still that hurt little boy that had been abandoned by his mother and neglected by his father.

"On that downer note." Jett cleared his throat and grabbed the dishes off the table, taking them to kitchen counter. He was trying to distance himself from all the truth bombs he had laid.

He was uncomfortable, and Selene could tell he didn't want to sit in the past. That was fine by her. But his confession had changed a lot for Selene. The fact that Jett had trusted her enough to share his past with her was a good sign.

It went way beyond the fact they were mates

and that they had agreed to be friends. He had given her a part of himself, and she was going to do something about it.

Selene walked into the kitchen and lightly tapped Jett on the shoulder. As soon as he turned around, she hugged him, her hands locking around his neck. She took a deep breath in, hoping her own energy could calm his. She was wishing that her positivity would seep into him and make him see just how wonderful it was that he had survived his past.

More than that, he was kind of thriving.

"You're doing great," she assured him. "You are second-in-command for the pack alpha. You bought a house and turned it into a home for more than just yourself. You have a community that trusts you with their lives. I'm sure there are a ton more things I don't know about that show how good a person you are."

Finally, he leaned into the embrace. Jett closed his arms around her waist and one of his hands pressed on the small of her back. He angled their bodies so he could look into her eyes, but that wasn't where she could feel his gaze. He couldn't look away from her lips. They were all he wanted, and that was made ever evident when he licked his own.

"Are you going to kiss me?" she asked in a whisper.

CHAPTER SIXTEEN

SELENE

*A*re you going to kiss me? Selene couldn't quite believe she had asked him that question. What's more, she couldn't quite believe Jett's answer.

"What would you think if I did?" His question made her heart tighten with hope. Or maybe it was another part of her that got excited.

"I'd like that very much," she answered.

She wasn't about to let this opportunity pass her by. Jett lowered his head and gently kissed her lips. Selene gasped softly, but she had an issue with the tender kiss he had given her.

Her hands behind his neck, she kept his head where it was, barely an inch away from her. This time when he went for her lips, he deepened the embrace, taking a good taste of her. His tongue delved into her mouth, and she did that little gasp again. The man knew how to kiss.

They stayed locked in a series of kisses for a long while. Selene could feel his erection pressing into her, and she rocked against it in hopes of taking this make-out session to the next level.

"Selene," he groaned against her mouth, "we can't."

"Why not?" she pouted.

"Because we've just met."

"But you're my mate," she argued. "And mates...*mate*." She wiggled her eyebrows at him.

He blew out a long breath. "I don't want to rush into anything. We've both been running on high emotions, and we're both pretty raw. We don't we just settled down and watch a bit of TV?"

Selene sighed and shook her head. "I can't believe I'm throwing myself at you, and you're rejecting me. Again."

Jett tipped her head back so he could look into her eyes. His own were stormy. "You can feel my cock. It's hard. Because of you. Because of your kisses. Me stopping us from going any further isn't a rejection. I just want to..." he licked his lips. "Deserve you."

"You already do," she murmured, not fully understanding why he wouldn't just give in.

He kissed her forehead and made his way into the living room.

"Pick the movie," Jett said as he passed her the remote.

Selene couldn't quite believe the gesture.

He wouldn't fuck her, but he was handing over his remote? What a weird move. For whatever reason, she had always believed men were very protective of their remote controls. It was a stereotype but it was one her only ex-boyfriend had definitely lived up to.

Jett was truly full of surprises. Not always good. She would've preferred a more naked activity, but she wouldn't push him. Yet.

Selene flicked through the choices, using the arrows on the remote to navigate. She couldn't quite decide if she wanted to choose an action movie to please him, or a chick-flick to torture him.

"I'm going with this," Selene finally said after scrolling through most of the streaming service's selection. It was a romantic comedy, but it had received rave reviews stating that it was actually hilarious. She could sure use a bit of laughter and a guaranteed happy ending.

If anything, she needed to be reminded that those existed in the world. It gave her hope that her own situation with the witch hunters would end in a good way. More than that, maybe seeing a couple happily in love would remind Jett those kinds of things were possible.

Jett settled onto the couch and he draped his muscular arm over the couch's back cushions. Selene was all the way at the other end of the long sofa. There was no chance he could touch her, but she could have sworn even his fingers were warm and pulling her in. It was like the entirety of Jett was made of something that called her. Selene wanted to explain it, but she couldn't. There was no way to, really.

Though he was handsome, and that sure as hell didn't count against him, Selene was also fascinated by his history and the way he chose to live his life. Maybe because she was a witch, and he was ignoring the mating beacon inside of him, *she* was experiencing the call. Was that possible? It wasn't like she could ask him. He didn't seem to be in the mood to talk about the mate thing. Not yet, anyway. She'd get him there.

The movie played on, and soon, Selene found herself laughing to the misadventures of the characters. She was completely pulled in, and she didn't realize Jett had moved much closer to her on the couch. It was only as the couple on the screen were getting their happily ever after that Selene noticed how close he was. And, of course, she couldn't be less sexy. She tried to wipe at her tears with as much discretion as she could.

"Are you..." Jett blinked at her, "are you crying?"

She continued to rub her tears away. "Nope." Her voice was shaky. "Not even a little bit."

"Oh, shit, you are." Jett shuffled onto the couch until he was sitting impossibly close to her. His arm wrapped around her shoulders and Selene let herself melt into the touch. It was comforting to be pressed against his strong, muscular body.

"I can't help it. Happy endings make me cry."

"Do non-happy endings make you cry?"

"Well, duh. They're sad. I don't like watching non-happy endings. What's the point of that? Life is shitty enough already."

"But you cry to both."

"Yes, but it's a different kind of crying. One is happy. Like, Oh! How beautiful. The other is sad, and I feel bad for the characters, so I can't help but cry."

"You're a fascinating person, Selene Bishop."

"Right back at you, Jett Arrowood."

The silence was heavy. Both were watching the other, waiting to see what would happen next. Selene knew what she wanted. She was desperate for another kiss. But instead, Jett leaned down and his hand cupped her cheek.

"I wasn't honest with you about what mating is," he whispered. "It means that you're my person. That I'm meant to spend my life with you."

Selene nodded. "I figured."

"My past doesn't exactly make me a good candidate for the long-term."

"Can we just take it one moment at a time?" she asked. "Maybe if we do it step by step, like dating, then the mating thing won't seem so big."

Jett seemed to consider her suggestion for a second.

"How about you ponder this," she added as she angled her body toward his. Her lips caressed his softly. The kiss was soft and tender, and Selene was trying to inject everything in it. All of the hope she felt. All of the things she knew they could have together if he just stopped being afraid of repeating his parents' mistakes.

"The way you kiss," he said against her lips with a growly wolf, "it's like everything else melts away."

"Good," she whispered before kissing him again.

So long as she kept their mouths fused, she could convince him they needed this. They needed each other. Selene was a firm believer that some people felt loved by hearing pretty words. Others only felt love by the gestures made. She instinctively knew Jett felt love with gestures. So she would do just that.

She would show him.

CHAPTER SEVENTEEN

JETT

Selene kissed him like her life depended on it. Not that he was complaining. At least his wolf had stopped losing his mind now that Jett was all tangled up with Selene. The wolf thought this was a good thing. That Jett would finally give in. That they would finally get their mate. The place they belonged. The wonderful future he didn't even let himself hope for, only during the darkest nights when he was roaming the pack lands in his wolf shape.

Selene stood and she tugged on his hand until he was coming to stand beside her.

"What are you doing?" Jett asked.

"What does it look like I'm doing?" she asked as

she let her hands roam down his body. He inhaled sharply when the tips of her fingers just narrowly missed the outline of his cock.

"It seems you're starting something." He was already hard enough to nail a post into the ground, but he wasn't about to tell her that.

"Well, good," Selene purred. "Because that is exactly what I am doing." There was mischief in her eyes.

"I don't think that's a good idea."

"I disagree."

Selene stood on the very tips of her toes and she pressed her lips against his. Jett immediately snaked his arms around her waist to press her against him. It felt right. She ran her fingers through the short-cropped hair at the base of his neck, her nails digging in a tiny bit.

"This isn't how friends kiss," Jett said against her mouth.

"Not really concerned about being your friend right now," she answered before kissing him again.

He knew he should stop her. But he didn't *want* to. What he wanted more than anything else in this goddamn world was to see Selene come as she rode his dick. He wanted to see her naked and feast on her delicious curves.

She seemed to be reading his mind, because Selene took his hand in hers and she slowly walked them toward the bedroom. In the room, she quickly turned on him to push him onto the bed. Jett hadn't expected it, and he sure had never thought that Selene, his Selene, the sweet woman who cried at the end of movies, would be such a wonderfully naughty tease. Her fingers hooked on her jeans' belt loops as she began to slow dance to slide them down her legs.

Jett couldn't believe what he saw. She was wearing hot pink boy shorts that framed all her curves just right. He would never pray for a thong again. This was the only lingerie he needed. Selene turned her back to him and she shook her hips side to side. The luscious curves of her ass moved beautifully. She looked over her shoulder and gave him a smirk before reaching for the hem of her shirt.

She gently pulled it up and off. Her bra matched her underwear. It wasn't designed to seduce, but that was exactly what it did. Jett wanted to leap off the bed to touch her. His wolf was begging for it inside of his mind. Even his cock was about ready to bounce out of his jeans, desperate for some kind of release.

"Selene," he growled.

"Nope, Jett. You always want control over everything, but you don't get to control this."

Still with her back to him, she unclasped her bra, letting the garment slide to the ground. She looked over her shoulder at him, and there was that smile again. She knew exactly what she was doing to him. Next, Selene hooked her underwear and she eased down the scrap of material. When she bent over, she looked back at him, and Jett could have sworn he could have come in his pants at the mere sight of it.

"Selene," he warned.

"Hush, you grumpy wolf. I'm having fun playing."

Oh, he would show her what playing was. The second he got his hands on her, he would show her just what it meant to play with someone.

Selene turned to face him, and there she was. In all of her naked glory. An angel made up of creamy smooth skin. Her blonde hair fell around her shoulders and everything about her floated as she made her way to him.

"Is it my turn now?" He wasn't able to keep the edge of his growl out of his voice.

"Nope," she teased as she placed her palms on his thighs. "I'm only just beginning."

Fuck.

He was going to die. She was actually trying to kill him. Selene reached for his jeans and she unbuckled his belt. Her eyes were glued to his while she slid the leather strap from the loops. She let it fall to the ground before her hands took the zipper. She took her time, letting her fingers graze him right where he was aching for pressure, for release, for something.

He had to lift his hips off the bed to help Selene slide his pants off. Thankfully, she also pulled down his boxers. There was only so much torture he could take from her. Her palms slid under his shirt and she tugged at it until he had to help her.

Then they were there, breathing in each other's air, and completely naked.

"What are we going to do about this situation?" he asked her, gesturing to their lack of clothes.

"I have an idea or two."

Selene wasn't done surprising him. She knelt on the floor in front of the bed, her hand grasping his very erect cock. She slid her hand up and down the hard length, her eyes glued to his. He opened his mouth to say something, but the words died when Selene closed her mouth around his cock. Her tongue twirled around the very top before she took him into her mouth.

"Stop," he said. Everything inside of him hated himself for making her pull away.

"Why?"

He didn't answer. There were no words to explain why he didn't want a blow job from the most beautiful woman he had ever seen. He closed his arms around her and laid her on the bed. Their mouths met in a passionate kiss.

It was his turn. And he would take it. Selene's desire scented the air in the most delicious of ways. He wanted to drink it all in.

He gripped her hips and pushed them down slowly. The look Selene gave him made his skin feel hot. With their eyes locked, Jett lowered his head and took a delicious swipe at her drenched slit. She tasted too good to describe. His wolf was already begging for more. He delved his tongue inside her, searching for the tight little bud. When he found it, Selene bucked off the bed with a surprised gasp.

He chuckled because she was already so reactive to his touch. He nipped at her clit, licking away the sting. Jett was aware that Selene was panting his name. It spurred him on and he kept licking her until her breath was so short, he was mildly concerned she would pass out. Her legs began to shake and then she was going over the edge. The orgasm made her pale skin blush in the most alluring shade of pink. Jett kept on taking swipes of her, reluctant to waste any of her pleasure.

"Selene," he asked as he climbed up the bed, settling himself between her splayed thighs. "Are we going any further?"

She arched her hips into him. "Of course. I want you, Jett."

He wouldn't be told twice. He ran the head of his aching cock against her core. He was teasing both of them in the best of ways, but he quickly lost patience. He knew what he wanted. He grabbed a condom from the bedside table and rolled it on.

Kneeling between Selene's legs, Jett felt like he had found his place in the world. Pleasuring this woman...*his* woman...was officially his new favorite thing. In his mind, his wolf was howling his agreement.

Jett slid is cock against her slit, watching her angelic face for a reaction.

"Fuck me, already. I want you."

With a pleased chuckle, Jett eased himself inside her. His groan was so loud, it nearly drowned out her moan, but he heard it. Selene was tight and warm and everything he had wanted her to be and so much more. He revved forward and jerked his hips, grinding down into her.

With every thrust forward, Selene kept her eyes on him, a naughty glint in the deep blue depths. Jett never wanted to stop. When Selene clenched her core around his cock, he had to count backward from ten to keep his focus. She was trying to make him lose control. And it was working. And he kind of liked it.

Sex had never been like this. It wasn't just physical. In this moment, it wasn't just their bodies that were joined. Their hearts and souls were connecting in the dance. Jett had never felt sex deeply in the center of his chest, but he did then. It was rewriting his history. Changing his future.

Selene was close, but so was he. There wasn't a chance in hell he would come without her, though. His hand reached down between them until he found the hooded shape of her clit with his fingertips. Selene shivered under him, her eyes rolling back as her gasps became breathier and shorter. She was close. She was right on the edge, and he wanted to feel it on his cock. Jett watched as Selene arched into him, taking all of him. She gasped his name, tightening around him.

Her orgasm was the most beautiful thing he had ever seen. He surged forward one last time, emptying himself inside her. Jett kissed her shoulder, so tempted to bite her, before disposing of the condom. When he joined her on the bed, he scooped her up in his arms and laid her against his chest. He was never letting her go.

Not after this.

"We did that," Selene giggled against his sweaty skin.

"We did. Are you okay?" Jett wasn't too sure why he had to ask, but he did.

He had never, not once in his life, had sex with a woman he cared for. This experience had been entirely different from anything else he had ever experienced. He held onto Selene tightly. His mate. His sexy, intelligent, sweet, funny mate. He kissed her cheek, inhaling her scent. It was completely her with a hint of him, and it made his wolf howl.

This was it. What his wolf had been describing. The feeling of being complete and at peace.

"I'm fine, Jett. Really. Why would you even ask?"

He swallowed hard. "I haven't really thought or cared what…" Shit, was he really talking about other women in his bed when he had his mate in his arms? He didn't know how to do this part. The post-sex chatter.

"Oh, so when you hookup, you don't care about them."

"Selene…" he whispered, feeling guilty and like the biggest asshole in the world.

"It's okay, I get it. I mean, I don't because I've only ever had sex with people I cared for. But we're mates, so it was bound to be different between us. Was it? Different?"

"Yeah," he answered with a low, raspy voice.

"Good. It should be."

Selene was kind of a wonder for him. She was an innocent looking woman, but she could be the naughtiest. It was a heady mix.

Tell her, his wolf egged on. *You have to say these things to your mate.*

Jett didn't know what else to do, so he took dating advice from the beast inside of his head.

"It's entirely different. I care a lot about you, Selene. You're kind of everything I've never let myself want."

She didn't say anything, but she kissed him. And that was saying a lot.

CHAPTER EIGHTEEN

JETT

Jett was very annoyed with a loud buzzing sound. It pulled him from the blissed out sleep he was currently locked in. He didn't know why or what the loud noise was, but it had to fuck right off. He was in heaven, and he had no intention of leaving it. His body felt happy and relaxed. That was probably because his hand was full of one of Selene's ass cheeks while her body was against his.

What was bothering him was the sound of his phone. Its loud vibrating on the bedside table was seriously messing up the tone of the evening. He grabbed the phone and barked into it. "This had better be good."

"You need to get down to the community center *right* away."

"What?" he asked, not understanding. He sat up, running a hand across his face. "Why?"

"There's been an act of vandalism," Carson said on the other line. Now that his head was clearing, he could hear the anger in his pack member's voice.

"What happened?"

"Well, don't freak out. We already put it out. But they had set up a pyre in the front yard of the center and set fire to it. It's out. And the damage is very minimal. They spray painted *witch lover*, *heathen*, and a few other things on the outside walls."

"Oh, shit." Jett and his wolf were both ready to wage war on whoever had attacked the pack's community center. "I'll be right there. Track any scents. I want the culprits caught."

"We're already on it," Carson said. "And before you ask, we already called Blaze to let him know."

"I'll be there in a minute."

Jett jumped out of the bed, feeling like a fucking asshole. He had slept with Selene, and now he had to run off in the middle of the night to deal with a problem. This was the last thing he should be doing. He should be basking in the afterglow with his woman in his arms.

But no.

Vandals had ruined the best damn night of his life. He almost let himself believe this was going to happen every time he tried to chase after happiness.

"What's wrong?" Selene asked as she sat up in bed. Her hair was in a disarray, and he wanted to smooth it down, proud and happy that he had done that. He had mussed her over. He had cast that rosy glow to her cheeks.

"I'm sorry, love. I have to take care of some pack business. There's been an incident." He didn't want to say more.

"What?" she blanched and leapt off the bed. "It was the witch hunters, wasn't it? Did someone get hurt? What can I do to help?"

"Nothing, baby. Get back to bed. I'll take care of it. It's my job."

Selene, who was still buck ass naked, crossed her arms. "I don't think so, Jett Arrowood. You are not going off to deal with a problem that I brought onto your pack by yourself. I am going to help you."

Fuck, he wanted to kiss her. It was so nice

knowing she was willing to be there to help. It was just too bad for her that there was no chance in hell he would take her with him to an uncertain scene. Now that he had a taste of what it was like to have a mate in his life, he wasn't about to put that in jeopardy.

"No, Selene. I won't be alone. There are already pack members there."

"I'm going," she insisted.

Jett gave her a small smile. Because she really was beautiful when she was all fired up for his pack. It made both him and his wolf extremely happy to see her reacting in such an intense way.

"I'm sorry, but you are *not* coming with me. You stay here where it's safe. Besides, there's no way of knowing if this has anything to do with the Order of Salem." That was bullshit, but he didn't need to tell her that.

"Oh? How many acts of vandalism has there been on pack lands in the last ten years?"

Shit. She had him there. She was way too smart. Jett should have known she would catch on.

"Well, none. But…"

"There's no way a kid from the pack decided to vandalize his community. You would all recognize his smell, right? So that would be really dumb."

Jett could only nod. She was right, of course. He already knew the witch hunters were responsible for whatever had gone down at the community center. He didn't really want Selene to know. He wanted to protect her. It was this deep, gnawing need inside him.

That's us, protecting our mate. That's what we do. Because we care for her.

It was as his wolf was talking then it dawned on him. He couldn't leave her in his home alone. That could have been the order's plan all along.

"You can go without me, and I'll just follow you." Selene shrugged. "Or we can go together. I'm going to be your mate, aren't I? Isn't this the kind of thing I'm supposed to be doing as your mate, anyway?"

Again, his mate was sharp. There was no denying it. "Okay. Yes. You'll come with me. I don't know if I would feel comfortable leaving you here alone without any protection, anyway."

"Good," Selene said as she started to grab her clothes from around the room.

"Just be prepared for what we're going to see. Don't let it affect you." He gave her a quick kiss and they resumed getting dressed.

It only took them a few minutes to rush to the

community center. The elders were already gathered there with buckets and flashlights.

The community center had been tagged with some atrocious slurs, condemning the wolf pack for siding with the witches. It seemed the Order of Salem wasn't too pleased with the existence of the wolf shifters either.

"I did this," Selene whispered, hugging herself. "This is my fault."

Seeing his mate's reaction made Jett angry and sad. It was almost too many emotions in his body all at once. He had to remember to take deep breaths.

Make sure she's okay. Comfort her, the wolf growled.

Right. He could do that. That's what he *wanted* to do. He just didn't know how.

"No, it isn't. Not for one second are you blaming yourself for other people's actions. You didn't put the spray paint in their hands. They did that. All you did was come into this world with magic. Just like I came into it with a wolf. That doesn't give people the right to do this kind of thing to our community."

Selene nodded, but her eyes were lined with

tears. Jett cupped her face in his hands and kissed her forehead softly.

"It's okay," he assured her.

She hugged him close and took a deep breath. "We have some cleaning to do," she said as she pushed away from him.

Selene picked up a bucket of water before making her way to one of the spray-painted walls.

"You don't have to help," he told her as he reached into her pail of water to grab a sponge.

Selene frowned. "Why in the hell would I not help? Your wolf pack is protecting me. This attack is my fault. The least I can do is help you all clean up. Besides, I like being useful and I really hate the idea that the kids will come out to play and see they can't because of this." She gestured to the vandalism.

Jett noticed the sadness in her eyes. He could smell it on her, too. Selene offering to help wasn't an empty gesture. She actually wanted to help because she was a good person. A good woman.

And she is for us, his wolf insisted.

Jett knew that was true. And he wasn't going to fight it anymore. He was still absolutely terrified that he would find a way to hurt her. That was the last thing he ever wanted to do. She meant too much to him already. He would have rather died than hurt his mate. Both his wolf and he knew that was the truth.

I won't let that happen, the animal said in his mind. *I'll help you keep our mate.*

Jett had to wonder if other shifters also took love advice from their animals, or if it was just him. He had a feeling it was because he was so clumsy with emotions that he had to rely so heavily on his animal instincts. Literally, he had to take his cues from a wild creature. He shook his head, hoping the wolf knew what he was doing.

Along with the rest of the pack who had come out to clean up the mess left by the witch hunters, Selene scrubbed at the paint. She hauled off chunks of wood, all working in tandem with the wolves.

Now that he was watching Selene interact with his pack, it did something to him. How was it possible that she seemed to fit in more than he did? Selene really was a wonderfully caring person. They were all seeing it—how amazing she was.

"Hand me that, would you?" she said as she grabbed the huge yellow sponge from his hands. "If I could do magic, I would spell the water to be even more purifying."

Some of the paint was stubbornly refusing to come off the brick. It would most likely need to be painted over.

"I would almost say that it's no use not doing magic," Jett said as he scrubbed at the dripping red letters. "I mean, the witch hunters already know you're here. What would a small spell do?"

"Deplete my magic and make it so I can't protect myself if they attack me?" she offered.

"Fuck, you're one hundred percent right." He kissed her forehead. "You're bright, Selene."

She smiled at him as if to say *duh*. It made him laugh.

He was very aware the elders were watching him carefully as he interacted with Selene. He had to wonder if they were passing judgment on him, on her, on them as a couple.

"Thank you for helping, Selene," an elder said, coming toward them. "It's so nice to see you here with us." The elder's eyes slid to Jett. For once, he didn't see judgment there, but mild curiosity. It made Jett wonder if he had been so locked up in the pain of the past that he had been seeing condemnation and anger where there was none.

Ding, ding, ding, his wolf chanted.

Well, shit. It was starting to look like his wolf

was a much smarter human than he was. How did that happen?

When you lock yourself out of the world, and I have to do all the work, his animal responded.

"It's my pleasure, really," Selene said to the elder. "How could I not help? I'm sorry for this."

"No need to apologize," Samson said with a smile. "You're not the bigot who did that."

"But I am the reason it was done," she whispered.

"No, not really," Samson assured her. "They were always going to come after us. The second they knew we existed, we figured they would come. It's what these people do. I'm just sorry that you witches always take the brunt of it. It's nice we can do something to stop history from repeating itself."

Jett didn't miss the look Samson gave him. It was poignant. Jett knew that before Selene, he would have taken in that comment very negatively. Now, he understood what Samson meant. He was just saying he was happy to see Jett getting settled.

He scanned his surroundings with new eyes. The entire pack, the people he had thought were against him for the sins of his parents, had come together for the good of the community. How could he have expected the worst from these caring people?

He had it wrong all those years.

And all it had taken for him to realize it was finding Selene.

CHAPTER NINETEEN

JETT

Hours later, once all of the mess had been cleared away and the brick painted over, Jett and Selene walked back to his house, hand in hand. Though the sun was about ready to rise, Jett felt invigorated. He was used to the late nights and no sleep. That came as part of the job of pack enforcer and bar worker. Usually, he would go about his day with a lot more grumbling and complaining. It didn't seem so bad now that Selene was by his side.

"How you doing there?" he asked he as she yawned deeply.

"Oh, you know me. I'm a late night party animal." She giggled, the opposite being true.

"You're exhausted. As soon as we get back to

the house, you're heading to bed." He spoke the order with care, but he had to wonder if his tone had been too bossy.

"No, please don't make me go to bed on an empty stomach." She rubbed the curve of her belly. "Between all of the sex and the cleaning, I am so hungry, I feel about ready to pass out."

Jett blanched. *Shit.* He knew she was prone to losing consciousness because of her low-blood sugar condition. How could he have forgotten that?

"I am so sorry, Selene. It slipped my mind. Are you okay? Do you want me to carry you to the house?"

She laughed and squeezed his hand. "Yikes, Jett. Don't be so dramatic. I'm fine."

"No drama here," he responded. "But I've seen you pass out, remember? I believe you were moments away from getting a Danish."

"I'll be fine. Though I do have to eat soon. Thank god your house is stocked full of all kinds of things. We won't be lacking for choice of breakfast."

"Breakfast?" he echoed.

"Well, yeah. The sun is coming up. Might as well just have breakfast and start the day."

Jett looked out at the horizon. The sun was actually rising. It had been such a crazy last couple of days, he wasn't too sure what day of the week it was.

"I'd love to shower," Selene said as they climbed up the porch steps.

"Good idea." He unlocked the door and motioned for her to step inside.

"Would you like to join me?" she asked with that mischief back in her eyes.

He had a hard time swallowing or forming any kind of words. *Say yes*, his wolf howled.

"Oh. Of course. I don't think I've ever wanted anything more than to shower with you."

Selene giggled, because they both knew that was a new need. But that didn't mean it wasn't a desperately strong one. Jett followed Selene into the bathroom, and they quickly stripped to step under the shower's spray.

It wasn't until they had emptied the hot water tank and that Selene was looking a bit woozy that they dried off. Both completely sexually satiated, it was time to take care of other needs.

"I know you're about halfway to passing out," Jett said as he walked to the kitchen. He took an apple out of the fridge and handed it to her after giving it a good washing. "Eat this. I'm taking you out on our very first date."

"You are?" she asked, her cheeks reddening in the most alluring way.

Droplets of water were falling from her damp hair. It was much curlier than he had thought, but he liked it. The wildness was very much on brand for Selene.

"Yup. I'm taking you to a diner. You're going to love it."

"What about the witch hunters seeing us?" she asked.

Jett paused a moment. He'd been so distracted with his mate, that he almost forgot she was in protective custody. "We'll be okay," he replied. "The diner is at the edge of pack land and mostly shifters go there to eat since we're on this side of town opposite of Salem. After all you've done to help tonight, they'll more than protect you."

Yes, his pack had accepted her as one of their own already. Guess they knew what he knew about her. She was more than worthy.

"So, our first date is a breakfast date," she pointed out as she walked to the front door. "Post-sex breakfast date. What a story we'll be able to tell the grandkids."

When Jett balked, she laughed with a very impressive eye roll. "I'm just joking. Now, let's go. I'm excited for this first date business. I haven't had one in years."

"And I haven't had one...ever."

Selene laughed again. "What a pair we make."

She wasn't wrong. They did make an odd pair, but somehow, that was going to be their biggest strength. Jett could feel the truth of that. Where he was a pessimistic grump, she was an optimistic cheerful person. They balanced each other, and he liked that quite a bit. It reminded him of the older wolf couples he saw around the community. It gave him hope for their future to think about them in their old age.

"I can't wait for you to taste these pancakes," he said as he turned the truck toward the main road.

"Umm..." Selene blushed all the way into her hairline.

"What's wrong?"

"Well, I don't like pancakes." She gave him a nervous smile.

His jaw dropped, and he knew he had to teased her about it.

"Wait. You mean to tell me that you adore cheese Danishes, but don't like pancakes?"

"Yes. But I don't see how those two things are related." She rolled her eyes.

"It's entirely related," he argue with a chuckle. "I put two plates in front of you. One has a Danish. The other has pancakes. You're telling me you choose the Danish every time?"

"One hundred percent, yes." There was no hesitation in her answer.

"You do know you're probably the only person in the world who would make that choice?"

"I'm unique," she said, beaming at him from her seat.

Selene was unique. And she was completely his. He needed to find the right time to bring up the full version of mating with her. He wanted to have these kinds of moments until the day he died.

"Waffles," he exclaimed. "You've got to tell me you'd pick waffles over a Danish."

Selene giggled and shook her head. "Nope."

"What?" he was genuinely stunned. "Is it the syrup you have an issue with? What about a banana split? Would that win?"

"Hell no. But if you put a chocolate sundae in front of me, you can keep the Danish."

"Well, at least that one makes sense. Any other thing I should know?"

She tapped her chin, deep in thought. "You already know I have low-blood sugar. You know I'm a cheese Danish aficionado. What else…"

"I know you cry at movies. I know you make a little gaspy noise when you're about to come. I know you blush everywhere, too. I know how you taste." Jett took her hand and dropped it on top of his thigh. "I want to know it all."

"Right back at you, babe." She winked. "You're the mysterious one, here."

"Fine. What do you want to know?"

"How do you take your coffee?" The question surprised him.

"Black," he answered. "Sometimes I'll add in a bit of sugar, but it's mostly black."

Selene nodded as if she were committing it to memory.

"That's it? That's all you wanted to know from your mystery man?" He gave her a bright, wide smile.

"Well, it's a start. That way in the morning, when I make my coffee, I'll know how to get yours ready."

Oh.

Well, shit. That was the sweetest thing he had ever heard. Selene hadn't just asked him about himself to learn things about him. Nope. His mate was way more caring than that. She had basically just asked how to do a little nice thing for him. It made his heart clench and he took a deep breath.

Now he really understood why Blaze had been so desperate to find his mate.

There really was nothing like this connection, nothing like knowing the beautiful woman beside him was always going to be there, ready to love him. He would honor that. He would cherish that. He vowed, in that very moment in the cab of his truck, to treat his mate like a queen.

Because she was a queen. The queen of his heart.

When Jett had first suggested they leave the safety of the pack lands and his house, Selene had been extremely reluctant. She didn't want to put anyone in danger, and she sure didn't want to see her man fight. She had missed the last time he had fought off the Order of Salem since she had passed out. But she wasn't up for a repeat performance of the fainting *or* the fighting.

But as it turned out, the diner was a great idea. The small restaurant was decorated to look like it would be open in the fifties. Selene loved the red vinyl booths, the checkered flooring, and the metal tabletops. It was like walking through time.

"This is adorable. You might have been right.

It's nice to get out of the house. Not that your place isn't wonderful," she added.

Jett leaned down and kissed the top of her head. "Don't go all motormouth on me, love. I know exactly what you meant. Cabin fever is a very real thing. We're still close to pack lands and I would never let anything happen to you."

"Okay," she said, leaning her head back more to give him access to her lips. He obliged, giving her a quick kiss.

"I need to use the restroom," he said, squeezing her shoulder.

Selene watched him go, his jeans-clad ass made her want to giggle. That was her man. She got to squeeze his butt all she wanted.

With a content, happy sigh, Selene sat back in the booth. How messed up was it that she was actually having a good time even with the threat of the Order of Salem hanging over her? She wanted to feel like a bad person, but fate had clearly intervened. How else could she explain that out of the four wolves sent to rescue the four Bishop witches, Jett would be the one to rescue her? Fate. It had to be. Especially because she was his mate.

Selene took a gulp of soda and as she was setting the drink down, a shadow loomed above her. Holy runway model. The woman had to be a shifter. It was the only way to explain just how gorgeous she was. There wasn't a single flaw or blemish on her face, and her hair was shiny and luscious like she was about to do a shampoo commercial.

The newcomer was giving Selene a very harsh onceover. It took all of her efforts not to tug at her shirt or hair. At least Mrs. Gellar's barbs had prepared her for this odd moment. Selene didn't move a muscle.

"Do you know who I am?" the beauty asked. Shit, even her voice was beautiful.

Selene sighed. "I'm guessing by your adverse reaction to seeing me with Jett, you're one of his lady friends?"

The other woman laughed dryly. "Lady friends? You mean, one of the women he fucks and dumps? I'm Leah." She said her name like she expected Selene to recognize it. She didn't.

Jett had told her about his reputation, but it wasn't like he had gone through his little black book with her.

"I'm sorry," Selene said. Jett was *hers* now, and there was no amount of bad looks and mean words Leah could say to make Selene change her mind.

"You think you know him. That you can change him. That he will suddenly be a one-woman kind of man. He won't. He will always have a wandering eye, and he will always be led by his dick."

But Selene did think she could change Jett. She did think he was going to be a one-woman kind of man. It was different between her and Jett because they were mates. He wasn't going to betray her or hurt her. Selene believed that.

"There's no need to be nasty," she said to Leah, hoping her voice was firm enough to get her to back off.

It didn't work. Leah laughed that nasty sound again. It was such an odd sound to hear coming from such a pretty package. Selene could only hope Leah wasn't really a horrible person. She was only hurt that a man she cared for was with another woman.

"You're plain and frumpy," Leah spat out. "If you think for one second you're going to hold his attention, you're in for a world of hurt."

Selene didn't know what to say. This woman was clearly going through something at the thought of losing Jett. That's something Selene could understand. Now that she had found Jett, she wasn't going to let him go. If she lost her man now, she'd be sad. Devastated, more like.

"I'll level with you, okay?" Selene said to the woman.

Leah narrowed her eyes. "What do you mean?"

"I'm Jett's mate."

As Selene spoke the words, Leah's face drained of all color and her breath caught. She couldn't help but to feel bad for her. Not pity, just understanding.

"Mate," Leah repeated.

"Yes."

Leah's eyes were lined with tears. "I guess it was going to happen eventually. I just thought..." she shook her head. "I guess it doesn't matter now. I'm sorry for being a bitch. I just..."

"You care about him."

"More than I should, obviously. I always knew we were temporary."

"I'm sorry," Selene whispered, meaning it.

"I was kind of hoping he would never meet his mate and that he would just settle for me."

The words surprised the hell out of Selene. "No, I'll have none of that." If Astra had said something like that, Selene would have pounced on her.

Didn't Leah have any sisters or friends who could help her realize that was a terrible plan?

"You can't let a man settle for you. What kind of life would that be? You will find your mate, or at least, find a man who will treat you right. Treat you like you're the most important person in his world.

"You're a gorgeous woman, and I don't know you, but I'm sure you're a good person." That was a bit of a lie since Selene's own interaction with her hadn't started out in the best way. But Leah was going through a heartache, some nastiness was to be expected, she supposed.

"You're being nice to me after I insulted you." Leah seemed genuinely surprised.

Selene shrugged. "No use being mean to others."

"Right." There was shame on Leah's face. "I really am sorry. And you know, you're not frumpy at all. I was just snapping."

"It's okay," Selene assured her.

With a nod of her pretty head, Leah turned on her heel and left the diner. Selene could have been mean right back, but to what end? She felt bad for Leah. It was never easy to see an ex with a new person. Especially if you weren't over them.

Selene took a deep breath and she let herself wonder if she would have any more run-ins with Jett's sexual partners. She sure hoped not. She could be kind and gracious, but there was a limit to how many reminders she could take of her man's past.

Jett was smiling at her as he was walking back from the bathroom. The smile made her heart do a few happy beats like it always did when he was around. He really was the most handsome man she had ever seen. It was no wonder the women he slept with chose to always go back for more, even when they knew they weren't his destined mate.

"Are you all right?" Jett asked as he took his seat in the booth across from Selene, obviously sensing her swirling thoughts with his shifter senses.

She gave him a small smile and a nod. His past didn't have to color their future. She had told him that and she believed it. It would be hard. It would be a challenge, but people could become better as they learned from their pasts.

"You look upset," he pressed.

"I just met Leah." She looked into her coffee cup.

"Fuck," Jett swore under his breath and he went around the table to sit beside her. His arm went around her shoulders and he kissed the top of her head. "I'm sorry, Selene. Really. I should have known she would pounce on you the second we were seen in public together."

"She's hurt that you're with me."

"She shouldn't be," Jett whispered with more force than necessary.

"Why not? I think she cared for you. Genuinely."

"What makes you think that? Because she reacted to seeing us together?" Jett seemed to be confused by the thought that Leah truly liked him.

"Yes. Absolutely. Also, she told me. Not that she needed to. It was written all over her."

"I honestly don't know what to say."

Jett looked uncomfortable with the knowledge that Leah had actually developed feelings for him. It made her wonder if Jett was still having reservations about being mated to her. After all, he still hadn't *actually* mated her. Maybe he was just waiting until she left, not trusting she could have feelings for him.

Going off her instincts, Selene placed a hand on his thigh. The point of contact was as much for him as it was for her. What she was about to ask him wouldn't be easy. "Can I ask you something? If we weren't mates, would you believe I cared for you?"

Jett took his arm off of her shoulders, and wrung his hands together. "What a question, Selene."

"I thought so."

She didn't need him to confirm what she already knew. He wouldn't have slept with her, and he wouldn't have started a relationship with her if it hadn't been for the mate sense. Jett was obviously still caught up in the belief that he didn't deserve love.

Selene didn't know how to change his mind. All she could do was care for him and hope that, eventually, he would come to realize he was indeed worthy of love. Even with all the difficulty she would have at accepting that Jett had had a series of meaningless affairs, Selene knew he had behaved that way from a place of hurt.

It didn't necessarily excuse the behavior, but she could have compassion for the wound that made him believe it was all he was good for. He had never been shown love, so how could he accept it or even recognize it? That would be the challenge of their relationship; Selene was acutely aware of that.

"I just want to make one thing clear," Selene shifted into the booth until Jett could look into her eyes, "I was attracted to you and thought you were all that and a bag of chips *before* I found out we were mates. Remember that kiss in the kitchen? I didn't do that just on a whim. I was having some very potent feelings."

Jett swallowed hard and looked away.

"You might think that because your mom left, because your dad neglected you, because no one really took you in that you're not worthy of love, but I am here to tell you that is bullshit. Everyone deserves love. It's basically a human need. I get that it's hard for you to receive, but hear me when I say I am here to stay. Even with all of the ugly that will pop up every now and then. That's just life, Jett."

CHAPTER TWENTY-ONE

JETT

J ett knew he shouldn't be this quiet on the drive back home from the diner. He should have been chatting away with Selene, but her comment at breakfast about the ugliness of life popping up had hit a nerve.

He knew personally just how much ugliness there was in the world. Had he met Selene under different circumstances, he might not have believed that she too knew just how shitty life could get. But she had been displaced from her job, her house, and her family because an order of psychos was out to kill her. She knew there were monsters that lurked in the shadows and that didn't scare her. She was ready to face them head on.

More than that, he knew she meant it. She knew she could take it. He was also very aware that they, as a couple, would be able to survive any rampage life threw their way because they had managed to fall in love during a very tense time.

The thought surprised him.

The *l-word* had just popped into his head, out of nowhere. He let it stay there; he let it slide into his heart. Yup. It felt right. How he had managed to go from not wanting a mate to falling in love with Selene in such a short amount of time was making him dizzy.

It's the mate sense, his wolf explained. *It's supposed to be this way.*

It had been such a heavy couple of days where life epiphanies were concerned, he did need a moment to compose his thoughts.

Selene had told him everyone deserves love, that it was a human need. Jett had never thought of it that way. He had always thought he didn't need any kind of human connection to be happy. He had always had to rely on himself and that had been fine with him.

But that wasn't true.

He had been lying to himself for years. That had been made all the clearer when he had seen his pack through fresh eyes as they worked to clean up the vandalism attack. He had built walls around himself to keep others out, and that had pushed them away. He had done it to himself.

To hear Selene swear to him that she was going to stick around, no matter what happened, had been a revelation. He had thought everyone left. That it was just life's pattern and he was the only one privy to that knowledge.

But he had been wrong. People had left him, yes. But others had been constant in his life. Blaze, Rick. Hell, even Carson had been a pretty big constant. Leah, too, if he let himself admit it. The reason he had kept hooking up with her was because somewhere, deep down inside of himself, he had been looking for that intimacy. He just hadn't known how to put words to it.

"If you do any more thinking, there's going to be smoke coming out of your ears," Selene teased as she hopped out of the truck. "You must be exhausted. How about we go in for a nice long nap."

Jett knew from the look in her eyes Selene didn't have sleep on the brain. But that was fine by him. He needed to feel close to her. He needed to feel her under him, he needed to hold her in his arms.

"A nap," he repeated.

She winked at him. "I promise there will be sleeping. Eventually. But you know, beds aren't just made for sleeping. There are other fun activities to do in beds as well."

"Oh?" he asked, smiling like the lovesick fool he was. How she always managed to flip his mood was magic.

"Yup."

Selene followed him into the house and before he could do anything, she had him pinned to the wall. Her eyes were shining and he knew something big was about to happen.

"Jett Arrowood, you need to leave that big head of yours and join me in the real world, okay? So I met your ex. Who cares? Everyone has exes. Even me. You had a shitty childhood, and you believe all kinds of lies because of it. But I just want to say one thing to you.

"No one can keep a Bishop witch under lock and key, or protective custody, if she doesn't want to be there. I am here because I like you. Because I choose to. Now, do me a favor. The next time you need to retreat into your head and think about the meaning of it all, let me be part of the conversation.

"Maybe together, we can change the lies you tell yourself to something more in line with the truth. That you have worth. That you're kind and awesome. Oh, and maybe, if you're really good, I'll even sing the praises of your favorite appendage."

Despite the seriousness of the moment, Jett burst out into laughter. What else could he do? She had taken years of fear and decimated them in a few short words.

That's the power of mates, his wolf said. *Now go make her scream our name.*

"I believe you had mentioned something about bedroom activities," he teased.

"I did," she purred, rubbing herself against him.

Jett wasted no time, he lifted her off the ground and took her to his bed. He laid her down and for the next little while, they were one. One body, one heart, one mind, moving together to prove that they were meant to be together. That what lay between them wasn't just love, it was a healing force.

They fell asleep, all tangled up in each other's arms. Jett let himself relax, knowing that this time, he wouldn't be awakened by his cell phone. Everything was going to be okay. His consciousness slipped, and he was under a warm, soothing glow when the sound of shattering glass woke him.

Smoke spilled in through the window.

He'd been right. It wasn't the phone that woke him.

The Order of Salem was at his door.

CHAPTER TWENTY-TWO

SELENE

The sound of a smashing window woke Selene in a fright. She sat up in bed, reaching out for Jett who was already covering her body with his. The room was quickly filling.

"It's tear gas. Keep your eyes covered and your mouth closed. Feel your way to the bathroom and wait for me there."

"What about you?" she asked.

"I'm a shifter, love. The gas will hurt like a bitch, but I'll be fine. Go." He gently pushed her off the bed.

Selene rushed to the bathroom and locked the door behind her. She felt silly for hiding while her man was out there fighting however many members of the Order of Salem that had descended on their house. She should have grabbed a weapon or at least gone to the kitchen to grab a knife. She rummaged through the bathroom, looking for something that would cause some kind of damage to any attackers who decided to bust down the door.

She had her magic, but she didn't want to deplete it and run the risk of passing out. That wouldn't be good for anyone. She tried to hear for any sound, but there was nothing. No sound of a fight. It was odd. There should have been *something* going on.

Even if Jett had turned into a wolf, there would be some kind of combat happening. The silence was eerie, and made Selene panic. What if something had happened to Jett? He was but one wolf against however many people. He could have been hurt, and she had run like a coward. Selene looked at herself in the mirror.

"You've got this," she told her reflection as she grabbed a bottle of shampoo from the shower.

The bottle was full and heavy. It wouldn't do damage to whoever she hit with it, but it might stun them a bit to be hit by a household item. She was sure she looked as silly as she felt as she left the safety of the bathroom. She aimed the bottle of shampoo ahead of her, ready to smash it on anyone's head.

She rounded the corner back into the bedroom, squinting against the tear gas.

No one was there.

Jett's clothes were still on the ground, but that didn't surprise her. She was sure he had shifted, and he had already been naked, so his clothes wouldn't have shredded in the transformation.

Confusion and panic were both begging for control of her reactions, but she didn't know which directions to go into. Confusion might lead to asking the right kinds of questions to find Jett. Panic, however soothing in the moment, might only lead to more problems.

Through the dissipating gas, Selene quickly slid on a pair of pants and a shirt. There was no way she was facing the Order of Salem buck ass naked. Next, she took Jett's phone off the nightstand and she quickly formulated a plan to head to the kitchen to grab a better weapon.

With shaking fingers, she scrolled through the phone contacts until she saw Carson's phone number. She hoped he would pick up and immediately get help to Jett wherever he was.

As she made her way to the kitchen, the phone kept ringing and ringing for Carson. With a large butcher knife in her hands, Selene felt a little better. She also grabbed a bottle of water in case she decided to do a bit of magic against the witch hunters. She slipped on a pair of shoes and slowly went down the steps.

Knife out in front of her, she felt just as silly as she had with the shampoo bottle. It wasn't like she knew how to use it. As she crept toward the larger community of the wolf pack, Selene tried Carson's phone again.

Voicemail. Again.

She could only hope it was because he was already helping

Then from behind, arms squeezed her against a chest, lifting her off the ground. As she thrashed against her captor, she looked around. She tried to get a good gauge of how many there were. Only one witch hunter was holding her. That was something.

They were alone. Good. That meant she could do some damage before he called over his idiot buddies. Selene closed her eyes and took a deep breath in hopes of aiming true.

With as much strength as she could muster,

Selene swung the knife past her side. The edge of the blade met with something soft, and Selene couldn't even think about the fact that she had just stuck a knife in someone's stomach.

She was immediately dropped. She lost hold of the knife, which was probably for the best. Whoever had caught her made a terrible gurgle sound.

"She's here!" the man yelled, his voice booming through the air. "She's getting away."

Selene looked back to see a man clutching his large tummy. She doubted she had done much damage to his sizable body. He was shouting dirty things at her, swearing he was going to gut her before setting her body on fire. She really didn't want to stick around to hear what other threats he could come up with. Especially not since he kept on shouting the witch was getting away.

Her eyes searching, Selene knew they would expect her to follow the road into the small wolf pack housing area. If she wanted to stay hidden, she would have to go deep into the small wooded clearing until she got to the water. The ocean was about a thousand yards away. She would have to run through brush, but she had to try.

With as much speed as her legs would allow,

she bolted for the line of trees. She had to figure that if she just kept running in a straight line, she would eventually hit the water. All around her the sound of snapping brush and shouts echoed through the trees. She could hear them, calling out profanities to her.

Chants of "Get the witch" were followed by "Kill the witch."

That was soon replaced by "Let's burn her back to where she belongs," and then, "Fire her up with the wolves."

"Kill them all."

Selene's heart clenched.

Nope. Not on her watch.

Her lungs were aching with the strain of running, but she kept on pushing, using all of the energy she had buried inside her. There was only one shot for her survival. She had to get the hell away from the Order of Salem and get herself to the shoreline. Now that the witch hunters were on the Marblehead pack lands, there was no reason for her to not do magic. She could do all of the magic she was capable of doing.

She just had to hope it would be enough to save her.

Finally, the sound of the ocean met her ears,

and she felt lightened. It spurred her on. She ran straight onto the rocky beach and into the frigid oceanic water, ignoring the cold and the way it cut her air supply as she stepped farther onto the shoreline. The tips of her fingers met the waves and she pleaded with the water to protect her. To rise and defend her against the witch hunters.

The pebbles and rocks under her feet began to tremble. That couldn't be good. Selene didn't want to cause a natural disaster, but she did need to save the pack. She needed to make sure the mob couldn't hurt anyone, witch or wolf alike.

The oceanic water was so cold, it was difficult for her to breathe. Her skin was pinching and aching from the frigid temperature, but she had to move past all of that. There were people who needed saving. *Her* people, both the witches and the shifters.

Ignoring the effect of the freezing water on her, Selene dropped to her knees, the water reaching her shoulders. She placed her hands on the ocean floor and closed her eyes. She knew that doing this much magic would be dangerous. Not just unsafe, but it would completely deplete her of magic for a while.

If she was going to do this, she had to make it

count. With a deep breath, she started asking the water to form a wave. She didn't know a spell for it, so she was just witch, kneeling in the ocean, begging it to help her save the pack and the witches.

The water was unmoved and unresponsive. The waves lapped at her back like she was nothing more than a silly statute sitting there. Like the waves could erode her away. But Selene would have none of that. She was a water witch, for fuck's sake, and she was going to use her magic to help.

Gritting her teeth against her chattering jaw, she inhaled deeply and spoke to the water again.

"There is danger," she said to the waves. "Danger that threatens me and the people I love. I need your help."

The members of the Order of Salem were running toward the water. There were so many of them. Just to take her away? Time was running out, and Selene couldn't feel the waves around her responding.

"Come on," she grunted. "They're right there, and they're going to kill me."

The ocean floor suddenly gave a massive groan and the ground shook so violently, Selene was pitched backward. As the water pulled away from the shore, it built itself into a large, threatening wave. It hovered in the air for a few seconds, a huge wall of solid water, sparkling in the sunlight.

As the witch hunters reached the wet beach, they came to a sliding halt, staring at the impossible sight. The wall crashed down on the shore, taking them and Selene into the undertow.

CHAPTER TWENTY-THREE

JETT

In the bedroom, Jett didn't know where Selene was. His ears scanned around him, hoping to hear the click of the bathroom lock. Nothing. He could only hope she had done as he had asked when he had jumped out of the window in nothing but his birthday suit.

His hands were up defensively, trying to demonstrate he wasn't a threat. If he could just move the fight away from the house, he could be sure that Selene was safe and out of their murderous hands.

"You need to leave these lands," Jett said with as much calm as he could muster. "This is protected territory."

"Oh, you mean because all of you are shifters? Dirty monsters who protect witches? You're all abominations. We don't want you in our towns, in our country, or in our world. We're going to pick you off, one by one, until there isn't a single one of you left on the planet to threaten us."

"We haven't threatened anyone," Jett pointed out. He was playing for time. He needed to see how many members of the Order of Salem were there before he shifted and started to fight. Strategically, he was at an advantage because he was on his home turf, but the witch hunters had their own edge. They were armed and they seemed to have quite a few more members than Blaze and Axel had anticipated.

Also, Jett was standing there, naked as the day he was born.

That didn't really give him any kind of edge.

One of the witch hunters pointing a gun square at his chest fired. Well, that put an end to diplomacy. At least Jett had done what he could to keep the fight away from his home and his mate. As the speeding bullet moved past his head, he crouched and let the shift take him over.

His wolf was pissed.

They had been having a time of pure pleasure. He was going to mate Selene. Then these fuckers had to interrupt the best moment of his life. He wasn't putting up with that shit. With the speed and agility of a ferocious killer, Jett's wolf pounced on the shooter. He aimed for the jugular and the bite landed just as he had intended. The witch hunter had gone for the kill shot, and he had done the same.

The man fell onto the ground, dead, and his buddies decided it was open season on the wolf. Jett bolted toward the clearing. If he could get the witch hunters to the small clearing, they would be far from Selene and far from the pack. Running with as much speed as he could, Jett took off.

He was followed by the humans who were wasting their bullets shooting at a moving target. He wanted to laugh at them for being so dumb as to try and shoot him this way. They would have been better off stopping and aiming. But they were clearly not concerned about killing him. They wanted the chase.

He would give them something to chase.

Jett ran and ran, feinting to the left. He knew there was a dip in the ground. When two of his pursuers fell with loud grunts and cracks, Jett knew they had been injured by the small trench. The three others were smarter and slowed to see where there was a safe path. Jett was watching them, deciding which one he would have to dispatch first.

But then, everything changed.

"She's here. She's getting away." The loud scream echoed, terrifying him to his core. "Everyone to the oceanfront. Now. She'll be trapped against the water."

He lifted his nose into the air to smell which direction the scream had come from. It was impossible. He was too far. He bounded down the high ground and doubled back toward the house.

He caught her scent and followed it. It was marred by the stench of the witch hunters. He couldn't see her, but he knew he was going in the right direction. He could smell her fear. When he saw the shock of blonde hair, his paws carried him with even more speed.

Selene.

He howled as he chased after the armed men. He didn't want Selene to draw the witch hunters to herself. He loved her for her bravery in the same breath he cursed her for being reckless. She might have magic, but she didn't have the instincts of a shifter. She couldn't rapidly heal from a bullet wound.

Even with powers, she was vulnerable. Especially if she did too much and depleted herself. Jett was also concerned she would pass out again. He hadn't forgotten how his mate had passed out the first time they had a conflict with the witch hunters.

Selene was running, her legs seemingly moving at warp speed. She didn't even look over her shoulder. Good, that would only slow her down. Jett knew if he sprinted, he could get to her. He changed course and aimed for Selene. His attention too focused on his mate, he was blindsided.

A shot echoed, coming from nowhere. Jett went down, rolling then slamming into a tree. In his right haunch, pain exploded, and blood gushed out of him from the bullet hole. It would heal fast enough, but it would seriously hinder his speed as he ran toward Selene and the rampaging witch hunters.

He stayed down, pretending to be dead as hunters rushed past toward the ocean. With one more bullet, they could take him out easily at this close distance. What good would he be to Selene if he was dead?

No one was moving around in the community anymore. It seemed all of the hunters were headed to kill his mate.

He ran through the pain.

Jett could only hope his smart witch could do some magic with the ocean. Maybe that was asking too much of her powers. He didn't know.

Reaching the tree line, he watched as the woman he loved ran straight into the ocean. The witch hunters began to laugh at her stupidity. They didn't understand what she was doing until there was a violent rumble beneath their feet. The sand shook, and the tide rode back at an alarming speed. The water was framing Selene, who was kneeling in the cold ocean.

Jett couldn't move. He could do nothing but watch as the oceanic wave went high into the sky, engulfing Selene. He howled for her, terrified she would drown. The wave, which looked terrifyingly high and powerful, crashed onto the shore, decimating the fleeing witch hunters.

No air made it into his lungs as he waited to see Selene. The water rolled out into the ocean before finally settling back as if the large wave had never happened.

Selene was nowhere to be seen.

Jett howled at the sky, rushing forward.

He couldn't lose her. Not now. Not like this.

CHAPTER TWENTY-FOUR

SELENE

Selene felt the water close around her like a warm delicious hug. She knew the water would protect her. She knew she wouldn't drown. The water wouldn't let that happen. She closed her eyes and let the wave carry her forward. The water moved under her, feeling very much like a water bed cradling her body. Soon, there was less and less water. She could feel the scratchy pebbles under her.

She opened her eyes and saw the wave had done quite a bit of damage to the shoreline. The witch hunters were nowhere to be seen. Slowly, she got to her feet. It was only then that Selene began to feel waterlogged and cold.

Her name being yelled out pulled her attention.

Jett was running toward her, naked and bleeding. His speed was impressive, and before she knew what had happened, she was tucked into a big wolf hug.

"You're safe," Jett said against her hair.

"Yup, all safe. All good."

He ran his hands up and down her body. "Are you hurt?"

Selene shook her head. She wasn't hurt, but she was two seconds from becoming an icicle. She was freezing and her teeth started to chatter quite vigorously.

"You're shaking." The worry in Jett's voice was nearly tangible.

"Well, yeah. Hypothermia is a very real thing. It's not like the ocean is a warm place to hang out."

Jett chuckled. "Right. I'll take you home and help you warm up."

"How many hunters are left?" she asked.

"As far as I can tell, none. They all came after you, and you..." he swallowed hard, squeezing her to him.

Just being in his arms was making a difference. His hot shifter body wasn't just *hot,* it was also as warm as could be. She nuzzled into his side and wrapped her arms tightly around him.

"You know what works really well for warming people? Skin to skin contact." She wiggled her eyebrows at him.

He laughed again. "You're impossible, Selene. We just survived an attack and here you are trying to seduce me."

"Skin to skin is the only thing that will warm me up."

"Well, then I would hate to be the cause of any pain for you." His eyes sparkled with love and lust. It made Selene dizzy, but in a good way.

Taking her into his arms, Jett rushed them to his house. Selene closed her eyes and counted every one of his breaths.

"You're hurt," she said as the house came into view.

"I'll heal very quickly. I'm a shifter. It's nothing more than a flesh wound."

When Jett set her down to help out of her boots, she was even more cold. His absence made her shiver, and she wanted nothing more than to be in his arms again.

"Skin to skin, remember?" Selene managed to say as her teeth continue to chatter uncontrollably. His soft, warm lips pressed to her temple in a continuous kiss as he carried her to the bedroom.

"Are you sure this is what you want?" he asked her.

Selene appreciated the sentiment, she did. He was being thoughtful and caring. It was nice, but at that very moment, there was only one thing on her mind. She had fought for her life, done a shit ton of magic, and she hadn't even passed out. That was a different kind of magic all together.

Now there was only one kind of magic she wanted to do and it was the dirty, naked kind with Jett buried deep inside of her while he made her come again and again.

She wanted to celebrate being alive. She wanted to make sure she took full advantage of her life. And that life would start with Jett. If he was her mate, then she would lean into it completely and take on that role. It wouldn't be any kind of hardship. He was hot, sweet, and wonderful. What more could a lady want?

"Maybe I should run you a warm bath. You could soak in it a bit and then we can see how you're feeling."

"Don't make me do another strip show, Jett, because I swear to god, I will do it. I will be a stripping block of ice."

"Why is it suddenly so important to get naked?"

his brow was furrowed and she reached out to smooth out the lines.

He was much more beautiful when he was smiling. Those rare smiles were only for her, and she wanted all of them.

"It's important because we just went through the fight of our lives. The entire time I was fighting, I was thinking about the mating thing. I should have pushed for it. We both should have. We love each other. We had sex-addled brains. Now, will you fuck me and make me yours forever or what?"

Jett's jaw dropped wide open. He wasn't breathing or blinking. He pretty much looked like a statue.

"Now, do you want me to be your mate, yes or no, Jett Arrowood?"

"Yes," he said immediately. He cupped her face and kissed her lips softly. "Yes," he repeated before kissing her again. "Yes."

This time the kiss was longer and deeper. His tongue traveled into her mouth, and Selene wrapped her arms around his neck to keep them completely connected.

"I don't deserve you, you know," he whispered.

"I'm sorry, but no. None of that. We have

already learned that is bullshit. You know you're not worthless. You know you have strengths, Jett. You don't need to keep telling yourself the lies you've been hearing and believing all your life. Love isn't about deserving. It's about receiving and giving. You love me, right?"

He gave her a nod, but his eyes were cloudy with the emotion. Selene could feel it.

"And I love you. So long as we keep on loving each other, treating each other with respect, and cherishing what we have," she placed her hand against his heart to demonstrate what she meant, "then that's all there is. You don't have to be the best man in the world to love, Jett. You just have to treat me right."

His licked his lips. "I'm going to forget that sometimes," he said.

It was her time to nod. "Yup. And I'll just have to keep reminding you. That's what love is, raising each other up when the other is down."

"I do love you, Selene. Are you sure you want to be my mate?" he asked her against her lips.

"Yes," she whispered.

"I don't have the best of histories. I have a checkered past."

"Stop trying to talk me out of this relationship.

I love you, you love me, and we are mates. That's that. It's final. I choose you, Jett. And I will always choose you."

He swallowed hard and slowly, his sad smile was replaced by one full of light and warmth. It did more to warm Selene than any hot bath could have.

Jett was quick at peeling off the wet clothes from her body. She was still shivering, but somehow, without the damp clothes pressing against her skin, Selene felt warmer. He reached behind her to unclip her bra, and the garment hadn't even hit the floor before he was closing his lips against one of her pebbled nipples.

"You taste like sea water," he said. "Not like you. We can't have that. Not if we're going to be mating."

Selene looked at him questioningly, but before she could formulate a question, he had picked her up off the ground and he was carrying her into the en suite bathroom.

"I don't want a hot bath," she pouted.

"We'll just hop in the shower real quick."

He turned on the water to the highest possible setting and helped Selene into the shower. He placed her directly under the spray, and she had to admit the hot water cascading down her freezing body felt really good. The air was thick with steam, and even that felt delicious against her skin.

Jett was running his hands all across her body, rubbing at her skin to help her warm up. He kissed the line of her collarbone before closing his mouth against her nipple. This time he moaned as he did.

"That's better," he whispered against her heated skin. "So much better."

Before Selene could respond, Jett was on his knees in the shower. He draped one of her legs over his shoulder, putting his face right at her pussy's level. She wanted to be coy and ask him what he was doing, but she couldn't find her voice. She knew just how good he was at giving her pleasure with his mouth, and all she could do was tangle her hands in his hair and hold on.

The first lick he took of her was slow and long, as if he were taking his time with her. He lapped at her with languid movements, never actually hitting the one spot where she wanted him. Had she had more leverage, she would have hiked her hips up for more pressure, but in this position, she was completely at his mercy.

When he finally sucked her clit into his mouth, Selene was mad with desire. He didn't just suckle on the nib, he ran his tongue alongside it. The suction and the feel of his wet tongue working her over was nearly too much. She felt her orgasm building inside of her core. It was making her warm all over.

Screw skin to skin. Getting eaten out by Jett was the best way to get over a mild case of hypothermia.

Jett continued tonguing her until all Selene could feel was his movements and the hot water cascading down her back. The intense tension of her orgasm was building and building, ready to snap. He knew it, too. Two of his fingers circled her entrance, and he began spreading her with the tips. The added sensation was all she needed to go over the edge.

Selene screamed his name, over and over, because that's all she could do. The release was powerful and everything she had wanted it to be. How Jett could have mastered her body so quickly wasn't a mystery. It was because they were mates. Because she was his.

Jett stood and his fingers traveled up her body until he was cupping her ass in his hands. He squeezed the globes before kissing her. How his tongue wasn't exhausted, she didn't know. But it delved into the kiss like it was the only thing he had ever wanted.

He turned the water off, but Selene didn't even have time to get cold again. He was right there to wrap her up in a large terry cloth towel. He rubbed her body gently, drying her off. It shouldn't have been erotic, but it was.

When Jett was the man touching her, everything was erotically charged. Especially when he was naked and his large cock was standing at attention, ready to get some kind of release. She reached out to the hard length and closed her hand around it. She stroked up and down, loving the sharp inhale it pulled out of Jett.

"That feels good, love, but I want inside of you."

Selene gave him a smile, and she knew he read lust in her eyes. That was all she wanted, too. He might have given her an orgasm with his talented tongue, but Selene was definitely ready for more.

Jett lay on the bed and Selene crawled over him until she straddled him. His erection was right there with a hint of moisture leaking from the tip. Her man was ready to go. Selene lined herself up and slid down slowly, watching Jett's face as she went. His breath was short, and his eyes were devouring her. When she bottomed out, she tilted her hips and it hit a spot inside of her that made her toes curl and her sex clench.

"Move, baby."

She did just that, rolling her hips in the most perfect of rhythms.

"Fuck, Selene," he growled. "Just like that…"

She did it again, smiling down at him.

"Just ride me, love," he roared.

And that's exactly what she did.

Selene moved her hips up, down; she ground from side to side. She leaned down until her breasts hung over his mouth and he was quick to latch onto one, then the other. Jett kissed every inch of her he could get his greedy mouth on.

They moved in tandem, just like they did everything else. It was perfect. It was everything. Selene scratched down his chest, leaving a few claw marks. He was about to mark her, but she wanted to do the same to him. She felt a primal need inside of her to make the connection complete.

"Will you be my mate, Selene Bishop?" he asked as he pushed her hair over her shoulder.

"Yes, please, yes."

Jett surged forward until he was sitting up and holding onto her. She continued moving her hips, but in this slightly different position, the angle was different and it made her gasp. She could feel her orgasm. It was *right* there. She moved and so did he, and there was no sense to their lovemaking. It was raw and primal.

Selene started going over the edge, clenching her core around Jett's cock, desperate to feel him come as she went down into her own passion.

He bit down on her neck with a roar, and pleasure erupted inside of her. Jett moved inside of her until he was growling her name. Selene felt him as he filled her with his seed. She smiled at the thought.

This was it.

They were mates.

Jett pumped his hips a few more times until Selene could feel him softening inside of her. He slowly pulled out and laid them onto the bed. His hand immediately reached out for her and he squeezed it before kissing it sweetly.

"You're my mate now," he whispered.

"It would appear so," she teased.

"I love you, Selene. I do. I know you said that I don't have to deserve you, but I want to promise you that I will always try my level best to make you happy. I want us to have a good life together."

"We will," she vowed before kissing him.

Jett quickly took control of the kiss, rolling them until Selene was lying on her back underneath him. She felt his cock hardening against her leg and her eyebrows shot up.

"There is no way you're ready to go again," she giggled.

"Keep kissing me like that, and I definitely will be," he answered before going for her lips.

Three hours later and a few more orgasms, they left the bedroom on the hunt for some food. Selene watched her man devour a snack.

Her heart felt full and about ready to explode with all of the happiness she felt. There was no way that only a few days ago she would have guessed her life would take this path.

It had.

She had been chased down by an order of murdering witch hunters. She had been saved by her mate. And now she had a whole new future ahead of her.

And to think, all she had wanted that fateful morning was a cheese Danish. Now, she had so much more.

She had a mate.

She had love.

"You're looking at me funny," Jett said as he swallowed his bite.

"Nope, not funny. I'm just feeling content."

Jett's smile was broad and it went straight to her heart. She felt breathless, but in the best way possible.

"You ready for happily-ever-after?" he asked her with a grin. "There's no crying."

"Only happy tears," she corrected.

"Only happy," he amended before leaning over the counter to kiss her. "Love you," he whispered.

Selene took the cookie out of his hand and bit into it. "Love you, too."

Jett protested with a laugh, but she ran with the snack, knowing he would chase after her. Knowing he would always come to find her.

Aweek after her life had settled down, Selene couldn't quite believe they were all safe. Just like her, her twin, and her cousins had all been attacked by members of the Order of Salem. Yet, here they all were, chilling on the back deck at Zane's house surrounded by the men—no, the wolves—who had not only protected them, fought for them, but were their soul mates. Their destined forever men.

It was fascinating, really. Fate somehow intervened on their behalf. Now, no matter what order of witch hunters rose against them, the witches of Salem would always be safe. Not only because they were now teaching and learning defensive magic, but also because the witches would always be tied to the wolves. They would always have protectors from the ugliness of those who wanted to kill all of the magic from the world.

Yup. It was a beautiful thing.

Almost as beautiful as Jett was sitting back in a lounge chair, his hand lazily drawing patterns on her thigh. The gesture was comforting and sweet. It was loving and tender. That's how Jett was with her. He wasn't the hardened little wolf who felt he had to fight everyone. He was a man who knew his past didn't have to dictate his future. Selene liked knowing she had played a small, subtle part in getting that particular change in her man.

The sun was beaming down around them, but they were sheltered by a large canopy. It blocked some of the heat, but it was still a beautiful after-noon. Nothing could compare to the joy she felt being surrounded by the people who mattered most to her.

She winked at Jett and he smiled back at her. The way it illuminated his eyes made her a little breathless. He would always make her feel this way. Because he was her mate, and because she was his. It was a particular kind of magic she wasn't going to question. She was too grateful.

The men had only just finished discussing if

enough steaks had been purchased for dinner, and it was only when Astra offered to go buy more that it was decreed that twelves steaks was indeed enough for the gluttonous wolves.

Selene was still trying to adjust to that particular shifter aspect. It was going to take a lot of clients at *Healsome Magic Holistic Center* and *Gemstones* to keep four wolf men well fed. She was positive her cousins and twin would agree to the expansion now. They would all want more free time to be with their mates. Again, Selene had to thank fate's helping hand.

"So, Sheriff Cross," Selene said, using that teasing voice she used when she addressed her cousin's man, "care to give us an update on the witch hunter investigation?" She needed to know, even if she knew her soon-to-be cousin-in-law had everything under control. Just like Jett was protective of her, Zane was protective of Raven.

Zane nodded, his arm draped across Raven's shoulders.

"It's as we suspected. The original members of the Order of Salem were far and few in between. Somewhere along the line, it became more like a cult and they let some shady people in. From what we've been able to gather, the founding members,

Mrs. Gellar and Mr. Griggs, only let the seedier people join because they needed people who were all right with killing.

"Some of the members we arrested weren't even from Salem. Not even from Marblehead. A few of the more problematic members were from Boston and had been evading arrests for a long time."

"I just don't understand how they knew where to find us," Raven asked.

"Ah," Axel nodded. "I can answer that one. when we found Billy hiding at Mrs. Gellar's home, we arrested him and he nearly peed his pants and confessed everything. Even the rest of the Order's plan for the other witches."

"Okay," Raven blinked. "How'd they know where we were hiding?"

"Honestly?" Axel rubbed the back of his neck and turned to Zane. "You tell her."

Zane grinned. "Billy seemed to have some type of sixth sense when it came to magic. At least, that's what he called it. He could feel it when it was used and could pinpoint it. The order had been on pack land, hiding and when Billy gave the word and where, they ran in. That's how they got there so quickly."

"So he was a psychic?" Raven frowned.

"Oh, no. He was very clear that was not what he was. He rejected the word immediately when I brought it up. He said it was just with magic and that was his only ability. The Order felt it was clear Billy was meant to lead them to find and destroy all the witches with this gift."

"Really?" Cerise grumbled. "So on him it's a gift and on us it's a curse? Assholes. And what about the other members? Were they all from nearby towns?"

"There were others who weren't even from this state. They were just people who wanted to blame all of their problems on the existence of witchcraft," Axel added. "But it's over. Everyone has been arrested and are going through the human's legal system."

"Those people were seriously messed up," Cerise said as she nuzzled into Axel's side.

"You're telling me," Blaze muttered. "There was an explosion in my bar because of those people."

Beside Blaze, Astra bristled with mock injury. "We all know that I and I alone was responsible for that tiny, little, itty bitty fire. And let's be honest, that bar needed a bit of a face lift. Really, I did you a favor."

"Oh, sure," Blazed teased right back. "Because seeing your mate explode is every shifter's dream."

"I still can't believe you were able to do that with your magic." Selene shook her head because truly, it was unbelievable.

It was so much more magic than the Bishop line had even been able to do. Selene knew how surprising it was since she had done her own bit of explosive magic to save herself and her mate from the Order of Salem. Only hers had caused more of a small deluge instead of an actual fire.

"Right. And no one was wondering how to make Noah's ark because of you." Cerise laughed. "I didn't get any cool magic like that," she pouted.

"Thank fuck for that," Axel growled.

"Hey," Blaze scoffed, faking injury. "That's my mate you're talking about."

"Better yours than mine," Zane said, agreeing with his alpha.

The group broke into laughter. The Bishop witches were still trying to figure out why one set of twins had been able to do more magic than the other. Their parents were sure it had to do with the fathers' bloodlines.

There was more magic in the Cory line of witches than in the Martin line. Alfred Cory, who was Astra and Selene's father, came from a stronger line of magic. That could be the only explanation. Joseph Martin, Raven and Cerise's dad, was also a witch, but his line was less proficient.

Selene laughed at the thought of all four cousins each having their own sets of twins. That would mean eight little Bishop witches running around wreaking havoc.

"What are you giggling about over there?" Jett asked her with a smile.

"Oh, nothing. Just wondering what our gatherings are going to look like when we start having babies and there are sets of twins running around."

All four wolves blanched and sputtered out different words.

"You *do* know that twins run in families, right? And twins are just a common occurrence in magic bloodlines." Selene shrugged because she had always known that fun little fact.

"You *had* to figure it was a possibility," Raven said, poking her own man in the chest. "You rescued two sets of twins who were cousins. Did you think it was a coincidence?"

"Plead the fifth," Blaze instructed with a big dopey smile on his face.

Jett shrugged. "I don't know. I kind of like the idea of twins."

Selene's jaw might as well have hit the floor she was so surprised to hear Jett say those particular words.

"What?" he said. "It would be fun to see what kind of magic they can do and to see if they turn into wolves."

"You know they'll do both," Zane said. "Because that's just how things seem to go with all of us. The wolves need the witches, and the witches need the wolves. It was true for us, and it'll be even more true for all of our little ones."

"He's not wrong," Jett said. "What are the chances that we all met our mates because of these lunatic witch hunters?"

"Well, I guess it was the only good thing to come out of the attacks," Zane said, squeezing his mate's shoulder.

"That's technically four good things," Raven argued.

"It wasn't chance," Selene said. "It was destiny. I really believe that."

"You would," Jett smiled at her before kissing her lips sweetly.

"Okay, ladies. I want some toasted marshmallows before dinner. Who wants to watch me start a fire with my hands?" Astra wiggled her fingers to the same rhythm that she wiggled her eyebrows. She pounced onto her feet and hurried to the nearby fire pit.

"No fires," Blaze gasped. "No explosions, either." He pointed a finger to Astra. "If you want, we can do fireworks, but I am not trusting you with a fire again. She almost burned off my eyebrows last time she tried a trick."

Conversations about what magic had been tried and the resulting misadventures came from all directions. With a big smile on her face, Selene looked around the back yard and her heart did a back flip. There they were, four witches and their wolves. They had saved the future generations of witches, all because they had fallen in love. Because they had come together.

She knew there was no way anyone would ever be able to come after witches again. Not anymore. They had their wolves, now. But more than that, they had their family.

The End... For Real This Time ;)

THE CASTERS & CLAWS SERIES

Spellbound in Salem

Seduced in Salem

Spellstruck in Salem

Surrendered in Salem

Get them all!

THE DAERIA WORLD

Check out the books in the Daeria World
The Nightflame Dragons
The Wintervale Packs

ABOUT THE AUTHOR

New York Times and USA Today Bestselling Author

Hi! I'm Milly Taiden. I love to write sexy stories featuring fun, sassy heroines with curves and growly alpha males with fur. My books are a great way to satisfy your craving for paranormal romance with action, humor, suspense and happily ever afters.

I live in Florida with my hubby, our kids, and our fur babies: Speedy, Stormy and Teddy. I have a serious addiction to chocolate and cake.

I love to meet new readers, so come sign up for my newsletter and check out my Facebook page. We always have lots of fun stuff going on there.

SIGN UP FOR MILLY'S NEWSLETTER FOR LATEST NEWS!

http://eepurl.com/pt9q1

Find out more about Milly here:
www.millytaiden.com
milly@millytaiden.com

ALSO BY MILLY TAIDEN

Find out more about Milly Taiden here:

Email: millytaiden@gmail.com

Website: http://www.millytaiden.com

Facebook: http://www.facebook.com/millytaidenpage

Twitter: https://www.twitter.com/millytaiden

ALSO BY MILLY TAIDEN

Nightflame Dragons

Dragons' Jewel *Book One*

Dragons' Savior *Book Two*

Dragons' Bounty *Book Three*

Dragon's Prize *Book Four*

Wintervale Packs

Their Rising Sun *Book One*

Their Perfect Storm *Book Two*

Their Wild Sea *Book Three*

A.L.F.A Series

Elemental Mating *Book One*

Mating Needs *Book Two*

Dangerous Mating *Book Three*

Fearless Mating *Book Four*

Savage Shifters

Savage Bite *Book One*

Savage Kiss *Book Two*

Savage Hunger *Book Three*

Savage Caress *Book Four*

Paranormal Dating Agency

Twice the Growl *Book One*

Geek Bearing Gifts *Book Two*

The Purrfect Match *Book Three*

Curves 'Em Right *Book Four*

Tall, Dark and Panther *Book Five*

The Alion King *Book Six*

There's Snow Escape *Book Seven*

Scaling Her Dragon *Book Eight*

In the Roar *Book Nine*

Scrooge Me Hard *Short One*

Bearfoot and Pregnant *Book Ten*

All Kitten Aside *Book Eleven*

Oh My Roared *Book Twelve*

Piece of Tail *Book Thirteen*

Kiss My Asteroid *Book Fourteen*

Scrooge Me Again *Short Two*

Born with a Silver Moon *Book Fifteen*

Also, check out the **Paranormal Dating Agency World on Amazon**

Or visit http://mtworldspress.com

ALSO BY MILLY TAIDEN

Sassy Mates / Sassy Ever After Series

Scent of a Mate *Book 1*

A Mate's Bite *Book 2*

Unexpectedly Mated *Book 3*

A Sassy Wedding *Short 3.7*

The Mate Challenge *Book 4*

Sassy in Diapers *Short 4.3*

Fighting for Her Mate *Book 5*

A Fang in the Sass *Book 6*

Also, check out the **Sassy Ever After World on Amazon or visit http://mtworldspress.com**

The Alien Warrior's Woman *Book One*

The Alien's Rebel *Book Two*

.

ALSO BY MILLY TAIDEN

Night and Day Ink

Bitten by Night *Book One*

Seduced by Days *Book Two*

Mated by Night *Book Three*

Taken by Night *Book Four*

Dragon Baby *Book Five*

Shifters Undercover

Bearly in Control *Book One*

Fur Fox's Sake *Book Two*

Black Meadow Pack

Sharp Change *Black Meadows Pack Book One*

Caged Heat *Black Meadows Pack Book Two*

Other Works

The Hunt

Wynters Captive

Every Witch Way

Hex and Sex Set

Alpha Owned

Match Made in Hell

Wolf Fever

HOWLS Romances

The Wolf's Royal Baby

The Wolf's Bandit

Goldie and the Bears

Her Fairytale Wolf *Co-Written*

The Wolf's Dream Mate *Co-Written*

Her Winter Wolves *Co-Written*

The Alpha's Chase *Co-Written*

If you have a teen or know someone who might enjoy the CLEAN and SWEET Crystal Kingdom books by Milly Taiden, try these:

The Crystal Kingdom (CLEAN AND SWEET)

Fae Queen *Book One*

Elf Queen *Book Two*

Dark Queen *Book Three*

Fire Queen *Book Four*

If you enjoyed the book, please consider leaving a review, even if it's only a line or two; it would make all the difference and would be very much appreciated.

Thank you!

Made in the USA
Columbia, SC
25 July 2020